Hal Brognola was in over his head

There were nine dead cartel crew on the kitchen floor. The nail hole in the palm of his right hand didn't seem to interfere with his shooting.

But now, he had less than a half clip of ammo left.

In the distance Brognola could hear a running gunfight. He wasn't the only one playing havoc with Samosa's troops. The other battlefront seemed to be coming closer and closer. Then he heard the hard crack of an explosion. From the sound, it was a hand grenade, no more than five hundred yards away.

If Bolan was that close, there was still hope.

Brognola steeled himself. He wouldn't let his old friend down. Wouldn't let him come so far, through so much danger, only to drag home some shot-up corpse.

MACK BOLAN ®
The Executioner

DON PENDLETON'S
THE EXECUTIONER®
DAWNKILL

Lord of the Seas
Trilogy

Book III

A GOLD EAGLE BOOK FROM
WORLDWIDE®

TORONTO • NEW YORK • LONDON
AMSTERDAM • PARIS • SYDNEY • HAMBURG
STOCKHOLM • ATHENS • TOKYO • MILAN
MADRID • WARSAW • BUDAPEST • AUCKLAND

First edition August 2000
ISBN 0-373-64261-X

DAWNKILL

Copyright © 2000 by Worldwide Library.

This will remain the land of the free only so long as it is the home of the brave.

—Elmer Davis,
But We Were Born Free

There must always be a struggle between a father and a son, while one aims at power and the other at independence.

—Samuel Johnson

To trust without hesitation is the greatest tribute to friendship.

—Mack Bolan

THE
MACK BOLAN®
LEGEND

Nothing less than a war could have fashioned the destiny of the man called Mack Bolan. Bolan earned the Executioner title in the jungle hell of Vietnam.

But this soldier also wore another name—Sergeant Mercy. He was so tagged because of the compassion he showed to wounded comrades-in-arms and Vietnamese civilians.

Mack Bolan's second tour of duty ended prematurely when he was given emergency leave to return home and bury his family, victims of the Mob. Then he declared a one-man war against the Mafia.

He confronted the Families head-on from coast to coast, and soon a hope of victory began to appear. But Bolan had broken society's every rule. That same society started gunning for this elusive warrior—to no avail.

So Bolan was offered amnesty to work within the system against terrorism. This time, as an employee of Uncle Sam, Bolan became Colonel John Phoenix. With a command center at Stony Man Farm in Virginia, he and his new allies—Able Team and Phoenix Force—waged relentless war on a new adversary: the KGB.

But when his one true love, April Rose, died at the hands of the Soviet terror machine, Bolan severed all ties with Establishment authority.

Now, after a lengthy lone-wolf struggle and much soul-searching, the Executioner has agreed to enter an "arm's-length" alliance with his government once more, reserving the right to pursue personal missions in his Everlasting War.

PROLOGUE

Osa Peninsula, Costa Rica, 1:20 a.m.

The shark's diamond-grit skin rasped across Mack Bolan's hip. The mass of its body spun him like a leaf caught in a whirlpool, dragging him underwater as it swept by. Sucked down into the blackness of the sea, dwarfed by the size of his adversary, Bolan didn't panic.

There was still room to maneuver.

Room to fight.

He grabbed the handle of his SOG SEAL 2000 knife, jerked it from its sheath and kicked to the surface.

Between the rise and fall of incoming ocean swells, the Executioner treaded water. Weak light from the blanket of stars overhead reflected off the half-submerged shark's back and tail fins. It swam in the direction of the dimly visible beach and the looming, silhouetted rain forest behind. From the distance between the two fins, he guessed the animal was at least fifteen feet long. The blade he held in his fist was just seven inches—designed for killing men, not sea monsters.

When a wave lifted Bolan higher, he was able to see beyond the shark to the lines of white froth and rising clouds of mist created by combers breaking on the sandbar in front of the mouth of the Rio Verde. The shrill screams of Samosa drug cartel soldiers trapped in the shallows had stopped. In the intervals between the crashes of surf, he could still make out the slap of shark tails and the splashing of heavy bodies.

The shark pack's feeding frenzy continued.

The beast that had sideswiped him turned in a big swirl and retraced its course. Its head was almost a yard wide. The shark accelerated, its exposed dorsal and tail fins sizzling as they beat back and forth through the water. The man known as the Executioner might as well have been tied to railroad tracks, facing an onrushing freight train. At the very last instant, he tucked himself into a ball, wrapping his arms tightly around his shins. The tremendous wave thrown by the shark pushed his body away from its parted jaws. As the fish savagely twisted, trying to snap a chunk out of him in passing, the side of its head slammed into his shoulder, knocking him even farther out of reach.

The massive jaws clashed shut twelve inches from his face, sending forth a gust of rotten meat–scented air. His right arm already coiled for the strike, the Executioner stabbed the SEAL-2000 with all his might. On contact, there was a split second of resistance, then the blade's point pierced the drum-taut skin behind the shark's gill slits. It scraped as it slid in to the hilt, scraped like it had been rammed into a barrel of fine sand. As the great head lifted part way up from the water beside him, Bolan glimpsed one huge, black eye peering sidelong at him. In the gloom of half-light, the eye was dead, expressionless. Blood the temperature of seawater, jet-black in the starlight, gushed over his wrist and forearm.

At that moment, he wondered if the huge shark had even felt the blow.

The animal answered his question with an explosion of breakneck speed. Instinctively, Bolan grabbed the knife handle with both hands. The shark bored out to sea, drawing him helplessly along with it. Letting go wasn't an option. Not while the shark was still capable of attack. The drag of Bolan's body as he was pulled through the water put enormous pressure on the buried blade. Almost at once the SEAL knife began opening a much more grievous wound. The razor edge sliced through skin and muscle, ripping a long, gaping slash down the beast's side.

After a few seconds, the shark realized that it couldn't shake free of its rider. It stopped swimming. Seizing the moment, the Executioner immediately put his knees against the animal's side and using all the strength of his arms and back, hauled the blade toward himself. The flesh parted easily and he could feel the knifepoint bouncing off ribs. The shark could feel it, too. It went berserk beneath him, thrashing and churning, trying to get its jaws on him. No way could Bolan maintain his position. It was all he could do to hang on to the knife handle. He slid up over the shark's back and as he did so, he carved a seven-inch-deep gash high along its spine.

Not deep enough.

Not quick enough.

The lashing tail smashed into him.

The power of the blow broke his two-handed grip on the knife and sent him sprawling. Momentarily stunned, Bolan sank slowly into darkness. At the first, burning breath of seawater he jolted wide awake. Choking, he swam to the surface, where he dog-paddled in a tight circle.

The wounded shark was nowhere in sight.

That didn't mean it had gone away.

Agitated by pain and the taste of its own blood in the water, it was likely to be close still, perhaps directly beneath him, preparing for another blindside attack. One that the soldier couldn't defend against.

Bolan had to get out of the water quickly.

As he started to stroke for shore, over the sound of the surf, he heard a sound that made him pause. It was the loud whine of an outboard engine. The sound was definitely coming his way. Then a high-intensity spotlight flashed above the tops of the waves, its beam spearing into the night sky. It was only visible for a moment before it disappeared below a crest. When it appeared again, sweeping over the sea, Bolan waved an arm above his head and shouted, "Hey! Hey! Over here!"

Immediately, the spotlight turned and pinned him. He couldn't see anything but its glare. Only when the boat got closer, circling to pick him up, could he make it out. The craft was a fourteen-foot Zodiac. In the glow of its white stern light, he saw a pair of men seated on the fore and aft thwarts. The guy in front aimed the bow-mounted spotlight down at Bolan as the inflatable boat pulled alongside.

"Get him in quickly, Marty!" cried the man running the outboard. He cut power and took the engine out of gear.

Bolan grabbed hold of the Zodiac's fabric with both hands. Written in big, black, block letters on the material was the name and home port of the ship the dingy belonged to: *Happy Landings.* Seattle.

The Executioner was very familiar with the *Happy Landings.* The night before he had slipped aboard the forty-seven-foot ketch as it had sat anchored some fifty miles to the south, near the Panama border. While its crew partied belowdecks, he had searched for and found the vessel's hidden cache of Samosa cartel cocaine. The next day Bolan had hitched a ride on a DEA surveillance boat that was masquerading as a Costa Rican long-liner, and followed the smuggling ship up the coast to the Osa peninsula. Less than two hours earlier, at around midnight, he had watched it unload its cargo onto a fleet of jet boats at the mouth of the Rio Verde. Evidently the ketch was still anchored somewhere out of sight, waiting for daybreak before it continued north.

Bottom line: It looked like the enemy was about to save his life.

Marty, a tall, bare-chested man with his hair pulled back in a tight, short ponytail, leaned over and gripped both of the Executioner's wrists. He was a very strong guy. As he hauled Bolan belly-up onto the port side's pontoon, Marty stiffened. "Oh, shit!" he cried. "Shit! Ken!"

"Bloody hell!" the driver growled. He let go of the outboard's tiller and grabbed for something on the plywood deck between his feet.

When the driver jumped up, Bolan saw the stubby automatic weapon in his hands. The muzzle of the Heckler & Koch MP-5 A3 swung his way. Caught half in, half out of the water, his wrists trapped in Marty's grasp, the Executioner grimaced as the submachine gun chattered, streaming autofire just over his head.

The bullets weren't aimed at him.

Twisting around, he looked over his shoulder. In the glare of the searchlight, he saw the shark. His shark, with the handle of the knife sticking out of its back and the long slash down its side there was no mistaking it. The shark swam parallel to the Zodiac, five feet away.

Ken held the trigger of the SMG pinned and raked the shark back and forth, from head to tail. Before the smoke and pink bloody mist could drift away, as quickly as it had appeared, the beast vanished.

Marty hauled Bolan onto the plywood deck of the Zodiac.

As the soldier rose to his feet, the ponytailed man asked him in Spanish, "Did the shark bite you?"

"No, but he tried damned hard," Bolan replied in English.

"You're American?" Marty said in surprise. He had a heavy Australian accent. His eyes looked wild.

Well-coked, Bolan thought. In the glare of the stern's

light, he could see the guy's torso was covered with tattoos, mostly the crude, blue-black, jailhouse variety. "Yep, I'm an American," he answered.

"You were almost fish food, Yank," Ken said, lowering the weapon and clapping him hard on the shoulder. From his accent, he, too, was Australian. Dark-skinned, barrelchested and hairy-armed, he had eighty-proof breath, but his speech was unslurred. "Lucky for you we were on our toes this night."

"That big explosion from up in the national park rolled us out of our bunks about ten minutes ago," Marty told him. "We were already on the deck of the yacht when we heard gunfire and the jet boats running downriver. We saw the boat's searchlights in the estuary, then they all winked out. What the hell happened out here?"

In his excitement, Marty had assumed that the man he'd rescued had to be one of Don Jorge Luis Samosa's soldiers. The Executioner didn't correct the mistake.

"The jungle camp came under a full-scale attack," he replied. "A few of us made it to the jet boats before everything blew up. As for what happened in the estuary or why, your guess is as good as mine. One second I was hanging on in the bow of a boat, the next I was flying through the air, head over heels. There were two other boats following right behind us. They must've flipped when they hit the sandbar, too, but I was already in the water, so I didn't see it. Awhile ago, there were screams from over that way...."

The two Aussies looked where he pointed, toward the shallows over the sandbar.

The truth was, the crews of the other boats had been chasing the Executioner down the Rio Verde, shooting at him after he'd blown up the Samosa cartel's main drug transshipment point, hidden deep in the Osa peninsula rain forest.

Ken stared hard at the shoreline. "Sure don't hear anybody yelling, now," he said.

"There could be men still alive in the water," Marty insisted. "We've got to keep looking."

Ken nodded in agreement. He turned the Zodiac toward the beach. Glancing warily over his shoulder, he alternately gunned and throttled back the outboard to keep them from being soaked by waves breaking over their stern. Marty swept the searchlight over the lines of foam in the shallows. In the bright circle of light, the sea directly off the river mouth was stained red with blood.

"There's somebody off the port bow!" Marty shouted. "At ten o'clock."

Ken steered in that direction, toward a man floating facedown, with arms and legs spread.

Marty bent over the side and reached down to grab the man's arm. Bolan caught hold of an ankle. They jerked the body against the gunwale, then turned it sideways and lifted. Where the drug soldier's belly had once been, there was a huge, ragged hole. His gray, uncoiled guts trailed down into the rust-brown depths.

When Marty saw that, he cried "Jesus!" He let go at once.

Unable to raise the limp corpse by himself, Bolan let go, too.

The body slid back into the water.

"Shit! Shit! Shit!" Marty snarled, wiping his hands on his shorts.

In the ring of the searchlight, the floating corpse suddenly moved, jerking underwater, then popping back up.

Like a fish bobber.

It happened again. And again. Something was chewing on the trailing guts.

"Bloody fucking sharks!" Ken said.

The Aussie wasn't paying attention to the sea.

A wall of foam from a breaker slammed the Zodiac and drove it sickeningly sideways toward the beach. Bolan had to grab hold of a thwart to keep from being thrown back into the water as Ken full-powered the motor. Engine howling, he got the bow cranked around and pointed seaward. They plowed over and through the top of the next cresting wave.

All around them, Marty's spotlight revealed zigzagging shark fins. The pack was still cruising the edge of the sandbar's drop-off. Off the starboard beam, the upside-down hulls of two riverboats drifted with the surge.

"We can't stay this close to shore," Ken shouted as they slid down the backside of another comber. "We'll get flipped, for sure."

"If anybody else was alive, we would've seen them," Marty shouted back. "They're either torn apart or drowned. Let's get the hell out of here."

Ken expertly angled the Zodiac up and over the oncoming swells. After they'd traveled a hundred yards or so, the seas flattened out and he opened up the throttle. As they rounded a small point of land, Bolan could see the *Happy Landings* in the distance, lighted up like Christmas. About a quarter mile to the north, its masthead, deck, cabin and cockpit lights were all ablaze.

In grim silence, the three men rode toward the anchored sailboat. Though Ken's submachine gun was within reach on the deck, and Ken and Marty were otherwise occupied, the Executioner made no move for the weapon. He was biding his time. To get safely back to Golfito before sunrise, he needed a bigger boat than the Zodiac under him, and the drug-running Aussies were considerate enough to be taking him right to it.

Ken steered for the stainless-steel ladder hanging over the ship's starboard side. As they approached the yacht, a pair of figures hurried out onto the aft deck. A small woman and a large man. The woman had on an ankle-length, sarong-style skirt and a tank top. Her long, mousy-brown hair was twisted into a loose knot on top of her head. The man was full-bearded, stoutly built and wearing baggy swimming trunks. In his right hand, he held an Uzi carbine. As Marty pinned the Zodiac's pontoon against the ladder and Ken tied off the bowline, the bearded guy leaned over the rail and gruffly demanded, "What happened?"

"Bad shit, Captain," Ken replied. "You guessed right. The camp up in the park got attacked. Three boats trying to escape wiped out big-time on the river-mouth bar. Goddamned sharks ate everybody. Everybody but this guy, here." He indicated Bolan with a jerk of his thumb. "He's a Yank."

"Go on up," Marty said, giving Bolan a shove from behind. "Climb aboard."

The Executioner mounted the ladder, swung a leg over the gunwale and hopped down onto the deck. The little woman smiled at him. Slender, tanned, with a face that was pretty without makeup, she would have been attractive if she hadn't been so obviously coked-up. And if he hadn't remembered so clearly what he had heard the night before on his below-decks recon of the *Happy Landings*: the sounds of sex coming from her cabin and the shifting, multiple partners.

"Who the hell are you?" the captain said, swinging up the Uzi. He pointed its muzzle at the middle of Bolan's chest. His thick index finger was tightly curled around the stamped steel trigger.

"Jesus, Captain!" Marty exclaimed as he and Ken joined them on deck. "Ease up a little. This guy just got his butt almost chewed off by a shark."

"Unless he answers my question, the shark's going to get a second chance at his behind," the captain said. He waved the Uzi in Bolan's face. "Who are you, Mister? Who sent you? And don't give me any bullshit because I know there aren't any Americans working for the cartel up in the park."

Bolan didn't say a word. The captain was on the verge of cutting loose with the Uzi; he could see it in his eyes.

"Can't we radio the camp and find out about him?" Marty offered, trying to defuse the standoff.

"We've been trying to contact them," the woman said. "There's no answer." From the small of her back, she drew a .380-caliber Browning BDA semiauto and racked the slide. "I think this big guy had something to do with the explosion."

"It could have been an air strike that took out the camp," Marty said.

"Only we didn't hear a plane," the woman countered. She leveled the small, blue-steel handgun at Bolan's stomach. She took a careful, barefoot step to the side, angling herself so the firing lane was clear. Her blue eyes were excited, almost frenzied. She wanted to shoot him in the guts and watch him die, slowly.

"I'm going to ask you one more time," the captain said. "Who the fuck are you?"

No way Bolan could make up an answer that would hold water. The yacht's crew already knew too much. And as far as his tactical position went, things were only going to get worse.

The Executioner had already measured the distances, visualized the necessary moves and the force required. Before any of the drug runners could react, he stepped forward and swept the Uzi's muzzle away from his chest with the heel of his left hand. Turning his right hip into the captain's groin, he locked his right elbow down over the surprised man's outstretched forearm. Bolan's fingers closed over the submachine gun's trigger guard, trapping the captain's gunhand in a grip of iron.

In a heartbeat, he had full control of the weapon.

Ken and Marty both lunged, trying to drive him to the deck with the sheer weight of their bodies. The range was barely a yard as Bolan squeezed the trigger.

As strong as he was, as big as he was, the captain couldn't stop the SMG from discharging. The Uzi in his captive fist clattered deafeningly and strobe light muzzle-flashes lighted up the grimacing faces of the two crewmen as they were jerked violently backward. The hail of chest-high Parabellum rounds lifted Marty off his feet and hurled him flat onto the deck, his limp arms and legs spread wide. Ken staggered, stepping back to the beat of slugs whopping into his torso. He fell against the gunwale. Before his knees could buckle, his momentum carried him over the side, headfirst.

As his body hit the water, the woman fired her pistol.

Bolan had already anticipated that. Tipping the captain off balance, he twisted the man into the shot, making him absorb the hit. The bullet slapped flesh and the captain moaned, his grip on the submachine gun immediately slack. The new target lined up, the Executioner forced the trigger finger down. The Uzi chattered and bucked, pouring a half-dozen rounds into the middle of the woman's chest. Spewing crimson from between her parted lips, she dropped to the deck.

The Executioner ripped the Uzi from the skipper's unresisting hand, ready to finish him. But the sailboat's captain was already dead. Without Bolan's support, he, too, slumped to the deck, a tiny, powder-scorched hole over his heart seeping red.

In the space of seconds, the *Happy Landings* had changed hands. All that was left was the cleanup.

As Bolan tipped the last of the corpses over the side, he

heard the sound of an idling diesel engine off in the seaward darkness. The slowly approaching boat had no running lights. He picked up the Uzi from the deck and held
it out of sight beside his leg.

Off the starboard bow, at the extreme edge of the yacht's
lights, the outline of a long-liner scow appeared. Its stern
was decorated with clusters of trash-bag pennants on long
bamboo poles. The shabby superstructure was made of
plywood and painted white. A clutter of miscellaneous
gear was bungee-corded to the peeling hatches and roof.

Bolan smiled.

The seagoing shanty had no name or identification numbers on its hull, but he recognized it and the man in a
stained cap and soiled cutoff jeans who stepped out of the
wheelhouse to greet him. It was Vorhees, the expatriate,
ex-Special Ops, who currently made his living by providing the DEA with intelligence on the coastal drug traffic
between Panama and Costa Rica.

Vorhees cut power and let the scow drift alongside the
yacht. "When I heard the Uzi go off," he said, "I figured
it might be you doing a little mopping up. That was a nice,
big blast up in the forest. You and Virgilio did the deed,
huh?"

"Yeah."

Vorhees looked along the sailboat's rail, then back at
Bolan and said, "Where's *el indio?*" He was referring to
his own deckhand, the local guy who had piloted the Executioner up the Rio Verde in a dugout canoe to the Samosa cartel's camp.

"I don't know," Bolan said. "I left Virgilio up on a
ridge with the Steyr sniper rifle. He did his job well. If he
hadn't given me cover, the cartel soldiers might've nailed
me."

"You left him with the Steyr SSG and the NOD?" the
expat said incredulously.

"Why is that a problem?" Bolan asked. "He also had the Heckler & Koch submachine gun and whatever extra mags and ammo were in my duffle."

"Shit!" Vorhees exclaimed, whipping off his cap and slapping his own thigh with it. He stared toward the beach for a long moment before he spoke again. "It's my own damned fault," he said. "We don't see first-rate, military issue pieces like that in these parts. Old Virgilio, he'll probably paddle down to the Panama border and sell the guns and ammo for cash."

"I don't give a damn what he does with them," Bolan said. "They were expendable, the price of doing business."

"Hey, I care," Vorhees countered. "There's a different kind of work ethic down here. Virgilio will bring back all the money he gets for the guns, then he'll marry some cute teenager from his village up in the Diquis valley and retire. I'll never see or hear from the little fucker again. Damn, he was a good cook, too."

Bolan let the guy mourn his loss for the better part of five seconds before returning the conversation to matters at hand. "I've got a very obvious crime scene up here," he said. "There's blood all over the deck. No way to sanitize it. Maybe we could take the ship offshore and scuttle it."

"Too much trouble," Vorhees replied. "We'll just abandon it at anchor. Trust me, the local police are so dumb they'll never figure out what happened. Not even if the bodies wash up on the beach."

Bolan shoulder-slung the Uzi and picked up the little Browning from the deck. Then he climbed down the ladder and stepped onto the scow's deck. Vorhees moved back into the wheelhouse and Bolan followed him. Inside, it was dim and breathlessly hot. It smelled of old sweat, diesel exhaust, cheap cigars, cooked garlic and stale beer. With emphasis on the beer.

Vorhees turned on his cabin and running lights, shifted the engine into gear and chugged slowly away from the yacht, heading south. Though bathwater warm, the breeze coming through the glassless wheelhouse windows felt good. It also cleared the sour air in the main cabin. When they were a half mile off, the Executioner leaned out the wheelhouse and tossed the pair of captured weapons over the side.

"I need to contact the States," he said as he ducked back in.

Vorhees waved at the makeshift chart table at the rear of the wheelhouse. "Help yourself," he said.

Though the long-liner looked like a death ship on the outside, it was equipped with sophisticated navigational and satellite-link communication gear, so Vorhees could report in real time to his DEA handlers. Bolan enabled the laptop computer sitting on the wobbly chart table. It took him five minutes to set up the secure, scrambled-data link with his home base, Stony Man Farm.

When all the security measures were complete, he started typing. In a couple of terse sentences, he confirmed the destruction of the drug cartel's storage site and gave the approximate time of his arrival at Golfito as 3:30 a.m. Then he transmitted the message and waited for a response.

After a scrambling delay, a string of words appeared on the screen in front of him from Aaron Kurtzman. "Roger that ETA, Striker. A plane will be waiting for you at the airstrip. Some bad news at this end. The safehouse in San Diego was hit thirty-six hours ago. We took one hundred percent casualties. Our man and the two boys were kidnapped by Murillo soldiers, apparently acting on the orders of Don Jorge Luis Samosa."

Bolan reread the last sentence. Shock and disbelief quickly turned to outrage. "Our man" was Hal Brognola, the head honcho of the ultrasecret Sensitive Operations Group at Stony Man Farm, Virginia, and one of the Executioner's oldest and closest friends. The "two boys" were the young sons of Yovana Ortiz, a Justice Department informant against the Samosa cartel who had been murdered in Tijuana, but not before she'd given up her evidence. The criminal organization of Ramon and Roberto Murillo, which had carried out the San Diego hit, controlled the Samosa cartel's drug shipments from the southern tip of Baja past the U.S. border. A little earlier, Bolan had watched Roberto Murillo, his captive on the jet boat that he had flipped on the Rio Verde sandbar, being torn limb from limb by a hungry shark.

"Why didn't you tell me this sooner?" he typed.

"It would have been counterproductive," came the reply from Kurtzman. "There was no point in distracting you from your mission. We had nothing concrete to relay to you until now. The kidnappers followed a highly complicated air escape route. After leaving San Diego, they took off and landed several times in Mexican territory, switching aircraft at isolated, private landing fields. They pulled this shell game over the better part of thirty hours, trying to throw any pursuit off the trail. The whole cyberops team has been working on the problem nonstop. We only just confirmed our man's current location, and the fact that he was still alive when he and the boys landed and deplaned in Mazatlán, yesterday afternoon."

"Do the Samosa soldiers know who he is?" Bolan asked.

"We have to assume they know he's important, otherwise they would have killed him along with the other agents in San Diego."

Bolan looked away from the screen. Through his network of well-paid informants, Don Jorge Samosa had probably discovered that Hal Brognola was the ranking Justice Department officer in charge of the Yovana Ortiz matter. He might even have known that Brognola was headman of the entire federal campaign to bring down the cartel, but there was no way Samosa or his spies could uncover Brognola's connection with Stony Man Farm. That operation was ultratop secret. Beyond even the reach of drug money.

What use did Samosa have for Hal Brognola?

Information, Bolan thought. Information about Justice's attack plan on his cartel. The trouble was, Brognola had much more dangerous facts than that locked up inside his head. Facts that could expose Stony Man Farm's decades of extracurricular black ops. Facts that could ultimately bring down the President of the United States.

The Executioner knew that Brognola would try to get away from his captors and, failing that, would commit suicide before the full truth could be tortured out of him. Killing oneself while in restraints and in the absence of a proper weapon was problematic. Just as holding out under torture was impossible. Having witnessed the grisly handiwork of Ramon "Three Nails" Murillo hanging from the blood-splattered wall of a Justice Department safehouse in Tijuana, Bolan knew that if Brognola was still alive, he was in desperate trouble.

On top of that, there was the nagging question of Ortiz's boys. Why had they been taken? Of what value were the children to Samosa? Their mother was already dead. They couldn't be used as hostages to buy anyone else's silence. If they were part of a message the drug lord wanted to send about the fate of informants and their families, why hadn't they simply been murdered in San Diego? It made no sense to Bolan.

More letters scrolled onto the screen. "Your ETA at the

KZ is 0815 hours. You will be fully briefed en route. Your mission is to rescue our man or confirm he is deceased. Standard rules of engagement are in force. Good hunting, Striker.''

The standard rules of engagement in the Executioner's theater were unique and quite simple: annihilation of the enemy. Annihilation by any means. As with the cartel's rain forest camp, as with the cartel's gold depository and its Hotel Flores headquarters in the Costa Rican capital, when the time came to tally up the score, the enemy survivors would be few and far between.

Hang tough, old friend, Bolan thought as he broke the satellite connection. Help is on the way.

Mazatlán, Mexico, 1:55 a.m.

The night's stillness, its humidity and sweltering heat lay upon him like a smothering blanket, making Trevor Eames labor for breath.

Except for the four other men sitting at his table and the half-asleep bartender, the hotel's beachfront bar was deserted. But for the shoptalk of his colleagues, the steady, low hum of the refrigerator and the whir of the ceiling fan, it was quiet. The cantina's raucous salsa music had been turned off as a courtesy to the guests in the rooms directly above, tourists roasted by the tropical sun and the excesses of the hotel's "Fiesta Night."

More times than he cared to remember, Eames had walked past the poster in the lobby that advertised the twice-weekly, fixed price, "authentic" Mexican buffet, which included complimentary pitchers of margaritas and dinner-show performances by a troupe of folkloric dancers and musicians. Fiesta Night was tailored to the needs of the culinary and culturally curious but cheapskate Germans, Italians and Canadians who made up the bulk of the Coronado del Sol's clientele. The steel trays of soggy tacos and soupy enchiladas had long since been cleared away, and the energetic, petite, dark-haired dancers in peasant skirts and embroidered blouses had likewise called it a night. Eames had no regrets about having once again missed the show. Bad food aside, he hated mariachi bands, the obnoxious, blaring trumpets in particular.

The former British subject, now American citizen, took another deep pull at his icy cocktail. The piña coladas tasted particularly delicious, as had his midnight celebration supper at a small *Zona Dorado* restaurant down the strand. The specialty of the house, which Admiral Oswaldo Fuentes had insisted he try, sounded utterly grotesque on the menu, but the gigantic, bacon-wrapped, blue cheese-stuffed, charcoal-broiled shrimp swimming in pure Vermont maple syrup were amazingly good.

Equally amazing, though it was going on two in the morning and he had worked straight through the previous thirty hours and now had four-and-a-half piñas under his belt, Eames was still wide awake. Everything around him seemed unnaturally vivid and intense. Smell, taste, touch, sight, hearing—all his senses were on maximum alert. This hyperexcited state had nothing to do with physical exhaustion and it had little to do with the victory he shared with the other men at the table. It was about a personal triumph, long dreamed of, now looming large.

Something unthinkably dangerous.

Totally criminal.

And immeasurably profitable.

Trevor Eames had spent the past two weeks at the nearby Las Cruces shipyard's dry dock, crawling around in the bilges of a brand-new seventy-yard-long drug-interdiction vessel (DIV). It had been necessary to get the sophisticated computer control system for its twin, 6000-horsepower marine diesels up and running by this morning's 9 a.m. launch deadline.

The discomfort he'd endured in the cramped, stiflingly hot underbelly of the steel-hulled ship wasn't the only minor distraction he'd had to come to terms with. That a $120-an-hour, software systems designer like himself had been once again forced to perform essentially grunt labor, inspecting and resoldering one by one a jillion, color-coded, wire-to-wire connections the Mexican electrical subcontractor had somehow botched, had made him livid. And only served to stiffen his resolve.

An incorrectly wired and therefore nonfunctioning sensor could have spelled disaster at the initial start-up of four million dollars' worth of Indexcon Marine engines.

Those concerns were history, now.

The power plants had been dry-tested without incident. In about seven hours, under Eames's continued supervision, the vessel would begin sea trials on schedule—an almost miraculous turn of events, considering the scope of the project, the hassles of working in and for a third world country, and the narrow time frame they'd been given to get the prototype ship into the water.

He drained the last of his drink. As he put his glass down on the table, Admiral Fuentes caught the attention of the sleepy barman and signaled for yet another round of drinks. The admiral was tall and heavyset, his crisp dress whites a stark contrast against his dark complexion. Both Fuentes and the uniformed man sitting next to him, Captain Ricardo Elizondo, had graduated from Annapolis. Eames noticed that neither Mexican was perspiring. He, on the other hand, was sitting in what felt like a puddle of sweat.

Both officers were highly intelligent, highly conservative professionals. From the start they had acted more like shipbuilding CEOs than military men. Which was entirely appropriate under the circumstances.

The Mexican government was deeply committed to the production of a fleet of state-of-the-art drug-interdiction vessels. With the help of hundreds of millions in U.S. taxpayer subsidies, and the technological support of U.S. corporations like Indexcon Marine and Eames's employer, Integrated Command Systems, the Mexicans would soon have four of the high-speed attack ships in the water, and they'd have acquired the ability to manufacture more. This wasn't just a hands-across-the-border crime-fighting measure, an effort to strangle the northerly flow of drugs. For the contractors and subcontractors, both Mexican and American, it was an enormously lucrative commercial enterprise. The Mexican navy and its government shipworks intended to market future production of their DIVs to other Central and South American nations, which, thanks to their own war-on-drugs subsidies from the U.S., could afford to buy matching armadas. The price tag was eighty million dollars per ship. Once the production came on-line, the commissions would be staggering for everyone but Eames, who was neither a salesman nor an executive.

The conversation around the table shifted from technical details of the impending sea trials to a new topic: how to extend the celebration further into the wee hours of the morning. Cal Albright, the Indexcon Marine representative, had some definite ideas on the subject.

"The raunchiest strip club in town has to be El Gato Negro," he said. "It's no-holds-barred." Albright was handsome in a craggy, pitted way, and he had a salesman's switch-on–switch-off smile. He'd worked with the Las Cruces shipyard on several other large vessel projects and, to hear him tell it, he was a seasoned hand at the seamy side of Mazatlán nightlife.

The fifth man at the table mopped his high, domed forehead with a huge, white linen handkerchief. From the expression on Bibi Ben-David's round, ruddy face, Albright had captured his full attention. "You mean, skin on skin?" the Israeli arms dealer asked.

Ben-David was supplying, among other things, the hardware and ordnance for the DIV's fore- and aft-mounted, Patriot-type missile batteries—a controversial add-on feature that the U.S. government hadn't officially sanctioned, but that it had decided to turn a blind eye to, for the sake of international relations and the successful prosecution of the war on drugs.

"More than you can handle, Bibi," Albright assured him. "This place is nothing but wall-to-wall sex." The Indexcon Marine rep flashed a leering grin. "Did you ever see that horror movie, *From Dusk Till Dawn*?"

Bibi gave him a blank look and shrugged.

"The one about vampires in a Mexican whorehouse?" Eames offered. Living out of hotel rooms 250 days a year while he did on-site work at major shipyards around the world, he got the opportunity to see a lot of bad movies on cable.

"Bingo!" Albright said. "El Gato Negro is just like the place in that movie. All its ladies want to do is suck and bite. And I guarantee they will turn you into a raging monster."

The Israeli had heard enough. "What are we waiting for?" Ben-David said, stuffing the handkerchief back into the pocket of his gaudy Hawaiian shirt. "Let's get out of here!"

"Is everybody up for it?" Albright asked. "Trevor?"

The expat Briton didn't have to think it over. In view of what lay on his plate for later in the morning, he knew he wasn't going to get to sleep this night, anyway. "Why the hell not?" he said.

"How about you, Oswaldo?" Albright said. "Care to dip your wick? Indexcon Marine is buying...."

The admiral frowned and shook his head. "We've got a long, challenging day in front of us, gentlemen. I don't know about you, but I need my beauty sleep if I'm going to be worth anything later on. If I crawl into bed in the next fifteen minutes, I can collect four hours of sack time before the launch preparations begin."

When this call to professionalism didn't dim the enthusiasm of his colleagues, Fuentes added, "Besides, I have more respect for myself than that."

The admiral's negative response didn't surprise Eames. He couldn't envision a guy like Fuentes, so conscious of the dignified public image he projected and the service he represented, ever stepping into a sleazy whorehouse, in or out of uniform. As Eames had discovered during the dozens of meetings before and during the construction phase of the project, the Mexican navy had a long, proud seagoing tradition, which its officers liked to trace back to the early Spanish explorers. And if the shipbuilding admiral didn't want to tag along on the little adventure, there was no point in asking his assistant. Without his boss, Captain Elizondo wouldn't go, either.

Fuentes pointed a blunt finger at Eames's wristwatch. "*Amigo,* if you're going to El Gato Negro, better not tempt fate. Leave the Rolex and all your credit cards in the hotel safe."

The barman then stepped up with fresh cocktails. Eames took his piña colada from the round enameled tray. Everyone else was drinking ice-cold Three Generations tequila shooters and *sangrita,* a spicy tomato-and-orange juice chaser.

Admiral Fuentes raised his brimming shot glass and said, "To cocaine! Without it, we would all be unemployed!"

Everyone laughed.

Even as Eames joined in the fun, a shiver rippled up his spine.

If everything went according to plan, in twelve hours the prototype DIV was going to lie wrecked at the bottom of some miles-deep offshore trench, never to be found. Along with the scuttled ship and the rest of its skeleton crew, Trevor Eames would be presumed lost at sea. No one would ever think to come looking for him.

What would these jolly, smart and macho Mexicans do if they discovered that for six million dollars in untraceable tax-free cash, he'd sold his soul—and maybe even their lives—to the Samosa drug cartel? Confronted with such a betrayal, the two naval officers, brave, strong, efficient self-starters that they were, would most likely seize the initiative, haul him out to sea, wrap him in a few yards of anchor chain and dump him quietly over the side.

As Eames laughed along with the others, an even less pleasant possibility occurred to him. If Fuentes and Elizondo weren't feeling particularly merciful, if they wanted to exact the maximum payback, they'd forgo the immediate gratification of his drowning and turn him over to the Mexican judicial system, which meant that he'd rot in a Sonora Desert prison for the rest of his life.

He took a long, steadying swallow of his pineapple-and-coconut-rum cocktail and assured himself the Mexicans didn't have a clue what was in the wind. And they weren't going to discover anything, either, not until it was too late. The alcohol burned like battery acid in his stomach and made sweat drip off his chin. All he had to do was settle back and hang tight. The ride from there was downhill. In a few short hours he was going to be drop-dead rich.

AFTER THEY SAID their good-nights, on his way out of the hotel with Albright and the Israeli, Eames followed Admiral Fuentes's advice. He stopped at the lobby desk and deposited the watch and his credit cards in the wall safe.

Beyond the hotel entrance's putty-colored concrete awning were four white jitney cabs. The customized Volkswagen Rabbits were touristmobiles, doorless, windowless on the sides and rear, roofed over with a sheet of gaily striped canvas edged with jiggly little balls.

The driver of the first cab in line dozed curled up on the front seat. Albright woke him with a shake and told him where they wanted to go. After a brief negotiation over the fare, the driver waved them aboard. With a chirp of spinning tires and a sudden lurch, both totally unnecessary, he accelerated away from the taxi stand.

Once they had passed the *Zona Dorado,* the beachfront strip that held all the big tourist hotels and restaurants, there was little or no street traffic. Their driver headed south, then east over a low hill, through the old, central part of Mazatlán. As they descended the back side of the hill they got a view of sprawling government-subsidized housing projects. Single-family houses, identical in shape and color, faced one another across paved streets. The treeless, shrubless lots were lighted by yellow mercury vapor streetlamps. On the far side of the housing projects were large industrial complexes, slaughterhouse feedlots, railroad lines and the highway.

The driver slowed as he approached a gap in a low, barbed wire fence, then he pulled through it onto the floodlit, packed-dirt lot. A dozen vehicles were parked in front of a large, flat-roofed, two-story building. It had mud splattered halfway up its beige stucco walls. There was no marquee, no sign indicating that this place was a nightclub called El Gato Negro.

The jitney driver stopped in the middle of the lot to let them out. When Albright asked him to wait outside an hour or so until they were through, he flatly refused. More words were exchanged, but they were too rapid-fire for Eames to make sense of them.

After the man drove off in a cloud of dust, Albright explained, "Our boy didn't want to come inside with us, and he didn't want to stay in the parking lot all by himself. He said either way, he was afraid he'd get his throat cut."

Eames couldn't tell whether this was the truth or just

more of the Indexcon Marine reputation for leg-pulling, macho bullshit.

One thing was for sure, though, in all his travels Eames had never seen doormen quite like the pair of overmuscled, crew cut, Mexican hulks guarding the nightclub entrance. Dressed in Desert Storm camo fatigue pants and tightly stretched white T-shirts with black letters across the chest that read Security, they both carried automatic weapons on military-issue khaki web slings. Their scarred and worn Heckler & Koch G-3 assault rifles had 30-round magazines. It was like they were guarding Fort Knox.

Based on the doormen's humorless, deadpan demeanor and their armament, Eames guessed that the whorehouse's neighbors didn't complain too much about the noise after dark. They either wore earplugs, or did all their sleeping during the day.

Though there was no notice posted, El Gato Negro apparently had an entry fee. Cal Albright, the bordello veteran, immediately reached for his money clip and shelled out the price of admission for everybody. Eames couldn't see how much cash changed hands.

One of the doormen escorted them through the entrance and across a dim quarry-tiled corridor to an archway, which looked onto the establishment's brightly lighted interior courtyard. Exposed to the night sky, the garden was where all the action took place.

Ahead of them, a series of concrete tables and benches bracketed a small flagstone dance floor. Along the right-hand wall, under an arbor of orange bougainvillea was the bar and the service counter for the kitchen. The odors of cigar smoke and burning joss sticks, spicy fried food and spilled hard liquor created a throat-etching, sweet-and-sour perfume.

Spotlights ringing the courtyard's second-story balconies poured light upon the small stage at the rear of the garden, beyond the dance floor. On the platform, ten brown women danced naked, jammed practically hip to hip, while the all-male audience that crowded around the tables at the front of the stage whistled and made catcalls.

Albright chose a table as close to the dancers as he could get.

Eames took a seat beneath an ornately framed black velvet painting of a long-haired blond woman and a donkey coupling. To his left, suspended from under the balcony was a TV monitor showing a porno film. More monitors were strategically placed around the courtyard, each running a different, but similar film. The dancers' salsa music mingled with the rhythmic grunting and shrill moaning of the video soundtracks, all of which was overlayed with the cheers and whistles of the customers. There was a definite testosterone frenzy in the air.

Scattered around the garden were more big Mexican security men. They wore large-frame revolvers in hip holsters and carried batons. Eames could see they weren't interested in the live entertainment; they were intently watching the audience, ready to come down fast and hard if things got too crazy.

In Eames's opinion, the barefoot dancers weren't anything to write home about. Short, with flat buttocks, floppy breasts and fields of stretch marks on their too-round stomachs. A floor show ripped from back issues of *National Geographic.*

Albright, Ben-David and the other customers, most of whom were Americans, didn't seem to notice or care about the physical shortcomings of the women. They had fallen into a trance. Eames had witnessed this phenomenon before. In part it was due to the combination of heat, humidity and the vast quantities of alcohol they'd consumed, but mainly it was the liberating effect of the third world. It gave these guys the opportunity to act without conscience or fear of consequences. To become animals.

Eames watched as the dancers hopped down from the stage and began to circulate among the audience. The women moved from table to table, servicing whomever wanted it, however they wanted it.

Eames looked over at the Israeli who was mopping his flushed, sweating face with the big hanky. The dancer was already laboring over his lap. Eames could see the top of her head as it frantically bobbed up and down. Under the table, the soles of her feet were black with grime. Up close, her brown legs were amazingly hairy. The sight made his skin crawl.

A mocha-skinned waistless woman with droopy breasts approached their table. She was apparently familiar with Albright's tastes. She produced a small glass vial and tapped out two lines of fine white powder onto the polished concrete tabletop.

"Hey, Trevor, are we having fun, yet?" the Indexcon Marine rep said as he accepted a plastic straw from the prostitute. He used it to quickly snort up one of the lines of powder.

Eames was once again finding it very hard to breathe. The smell of the cheap perfume that the two whores had doused themselves in wasn't helping the situation, either.

Wiping the white dust from the tip of his nose, Albright picked up a menu card. "Anybody else hungry?" he said. "I don't know about you guys, but I'm in the mood for some monkey tacos."

Trevor got a mental image of monkey brains dripping out both sides of an overstuffed, fried tortilla shell. It put him right over the edge. Suddenly queasy, he bolted up from his chair. "Got to get some air," he muttered, and made for the exit.

The doormen paid him no mind as he staggered past

them. Out in the parking lot, he leaned against the side of an SUV, palms flat on a fender, head hanging down. His stomach convulsed, but his throat remained clamped shut. He dry-heaved over and over. When the spasms passed, he straightened, groaning, strands of saliva swaying from his parted lips.

"You probably shouldn't drink so much," a familiar voice said softly from behind him.

Eames looked over his shoulder.

A tall man with white hair slicked straight back was smiling at him. He wore a pale-yellow guayabera shirt, loose-fitting slacks and leather fisherman's sandals.

"You followed me here?" Eames said. "What do you want?"

"I'm just looking after Don Jorge Samosa's investment."

Eames wiped his mouth and chin with the back of his hand. He had met Joseph Crecca at the Coronado del Sol's bar many months earlier, when the DIV project was still in the early stages. At first their meeting had seemed accidental, but it turned out to be no accident. Crecca said he was involved in Latin American "agribusiness." Eames didn't find out for weeks that the cultivated product the white-haired man brokered was cocaine.

Samosa cartel cocaine.

Why had the drug cartel decided to focus solely on him? Because it couldn't rely on any of the Mexicans to do the job. None of them knew enough about the computer control system to operate the DIV. Eames knew everything, so he was the only logical choice.

As for Crecca, he knew how to play on long-festering resentments. After gaining Eames's confidence, the expat Briton gradually revealed to him his unspoken, unfulfilled desires, of how tired Eames was of working on other people's ships—rich people's ships—and of how he wanted

everything they had. And that he wanted it all, without
further delay.

"I came here to deliver a message," Crecca said. "If
anything goes wrong later, you're going to be dead."

Trevor blinked at him.

"If you change your mind, if you warn your Mexican
navy friends, you're meat. The Lord of the Seas will spare
no expense to hunt you down. Your dying will not be
quick or easy. Do you understand?"

Eames grimaced.

"Do you understand?"

The software system designer nodded stiffly.

"Good night, my friend."

As Crecca turned away, Eames threw up.

2

Village of Corto de Vista, Mexico, 7:50 a.m.

Morning sun streamed into the white-walled room through tall, curtainless windows. The longest night of Hal Brognola's life was over. The longest day had begun.

He stood perched on the room's only piece of furniture, an orange crate, his back pressed flat against the wall. He had been in this position since the previous afternoon, unable to step down from the box because of the spike driven through the palm of his right hand and into the stud behind the Sheetrock. The nail had been placed perfectly between the radiating bones of his hand and wrist. The head of the spike was wide, the diameter of a nickel. To rip it free meant breaking many bones.

When his torturers had finally left him, in the small hours of the morning, he had tried desperately to enlarge the hole by pulling down and pushing up on his hand as hard as he could. The resulting pain made him black out short of his goal. He came to sometime later, his body weight hanging from the buried spike, his upraised arm encrusted with dried blood.

The impaled hand had become horribly swollen, its rigid, clawlike fingers purple and bruised. His right arm throbbed agonizingly from wrist to shoulder.

For a while he'd thought for sure the drug soldiers were going to do the whole number on him: Ramon Murillo's infamous three-nail trick. Gradually, he realized that that wasn't going to be the case. After the hours-long interrogation session, they'd just left him stuck there, helpless, like a bug on a pin. Left him to dwell on what was to come.

It was all part of a tried-and-true torture technique. The idea wasn't to take the prisoner past the point of no return. At a certain stage of physical destruction, a victim loses hope and decides that given the permanent injuries he or she has suffered, death is preferable to life. When all hope of recovery is lost, getting information from a prisoner becomes more difficult, perhaps even impossible since withholding it is the only power, the only revenge the victim has.

The cartel interrogation crew, under the direction of Ramon Murillo, had been highly professional, his sick reputation notwithstanding. They had pounded him with their fists and kicked him some, but it was light punishment as beatings went, and he had only lost consciousness a couple of times. Perhaps this was because Don Jorge Luis Samosa was in the room for most of the questioning, monitoring things.

Crucifixion was Ramon Murillo's speciality, his murderous trademark, although he rarely used an actual cross to facilitate matters. More often than not, he relied on flat surfaces, interior walls, garage doors, high wooden fences. Crucifixion was a very bad way to die. Due to the position of the body and its considerable deadweight hanging from the stapled hands, the victim soon became exhausted, unable to keep his head up, to keep the windpipe open. As a result, the crucified person slowly suffocated.

With just one arm nailed up, and the resulting cramps in his shoulders and back, Brognola had already glimpsed what lay ahead for him. The interrogators would put off that end as long as possible. Once all three nails were pounded in, there was no place further to take him, torture-wise. No additional threat, no new horror, nothing to use to manipulate him. They would repeat their questions until he either answered them or expired.

The big Fed already knew the shortlist of questions by heart.

Who is the operative who hit the Hotel Flores and the *Paniagua* gold depository? Who killed all of Samosa's Costa Rican lieutenants and exposed his secret treasure of bullion to confiscation by that government?

Over and over, like a tape loop.

Who is the man?

Who is controlling him?

Where will he strike next?

Brognola could provide them with none of the desired answers. They were like a row of tightly spaced dominoes, tip just one over and all the rest would come crashing down. The world would come down. Knowing who the Executioner was, his name, the particulars of his dossier, wouldn't help the cartel defend itself against him, but Brognola couldn't tell them that. And he had no idea where Mack Bolan was going to hit next. If Brognola began giving even useless answers, in short order Stony Man Farm would be compromised and the President of the United States would be crippled. That was the way torture worked. Once he started talking to end the pain, he wouldn't stop. The floodgates of truth inevitably opened wide, then it was just a matter of time and precisely applied pressure. When that happened, everything that Brognola had worked for in his long and distinguished career would go down the crapper. It would all end in disgrace and dishonor, misinterpreted by some congressional investigative committee. Everyone involved in the covert operation would be publicly shamed, hounded from office, if not jailed for a very long time.

At around four o'clock the torture crew had received some sketchy news about the Executioner's attack on the Osa peninsula drug depot, about the horrible loss of life and the destruction of a hundred million dollars' worth of cartel cocaine. When Ramon Murillo got the word that his half brother, Roberto, who had been at the rain forest camp, was perhaps dead or injured, he didn't take it well. It was at that point that Samosa broke off the interrogation. There was nothing more to be gained by continuing, and so much to lose. Murillo was clearly too upset to control himself.

Brognola stared at the tall windows, the azure sky beyond, certain that his time was running out. As the only federal law enforcement officer to ever see Don Jorge Luis Samosa face-to-face, he was under a death sentence. A rescue attempt wasn't completely out of the question, but its success depended on many variables. Could Bolan arrive on the scene and get to him before Ramon Murillo turned up the heat on the inquisition? Before the torture finally broke him? There was no guarantee of that.

Scant options remained.

Brognola didn't have a cyanide-filled false tooth. Samosa's men had taken his belt. His shoes didn't have laces. His duty to his nation, to his President, to the men and women of Stony Man Farm, and to their mission, required that he take his own life. The big Fed had no illusions about his importance; he was replaceable. If the Farm's secrecy was compromised, however, it could never get it back. Game over.

He stared at his left wrist, at the blue veins that looped under the sheaf of tendons there. He had no sharp edge to make the necessary deep cut. Even if he broke a window by tossing one of his shoes at it, the spike would keep him from reaching the fallen shards of glass.

Improvise.

Brognola tested his wrist against his parted teeth. The tendons blocked access to the veins, which rolled out of the way. He knew he wouldn't be able to do it with just one bite. It would take many bites to get through the skin and to the veins. A successful suicide attempt was going to be a long, painful and messy process, no doubt about it.

He shut his eyes, steeling himself for what he had to do. He was filled with a crushing sadness. He had left so many things unsaid, to his wife, his children, his close friends; and he had left many important tasks unfinished. He didn't want to die by his own hand. He didn't want to die at all. There was no time to dwell on it. If he put off the deed any longer, he risked not getting it done. If Murillo and the others came back and finished nailing him up, he'd be left with an even less pleasant option: to try to swallow his own tongue. It was a much more difficult and painful feat, demanding an even greater test of physical control and sheer willpower.

At the sound of the door latch clicking back, Brognola looked up, thinking with a sinking heart that his interrogators had already returned. The door swung inward a couple of inches. The big brown eyes that peered at him through the crack were at what would have been his midchest height.

"Juanito, come in!" Brognola said to the boy. "Come in, quickly! Before someone sees you."

Yovana Ortiz's son wasn't alone. His little brother, Pedro, was with him. Both boys stepped into the bright room. They stared wide-eyed at his right hand, the nail and all the blood.

"Shut the door," Brognola told them in a low voice. When they had done that, he said, "Are you boys all right?"

Juanito nodded. "We're fine." Then he pointed at the injured hand and said, "Ramon did that to you?"

"That's right."

"It looks like it hurts," Pedro said.

"Yes, it does."

"You must've done something real bad," Pedro said.

"No, I didn't," Brognola insisted. "There's been a mistake, a terrible mistake. No one will listen to me. You boys know who I am. You know I've tried to help you and your mother. I've done my best to protect all of you. I'm the one that needs the help, now, to get free of this."

Juanito eyeballed the distances involved. "I can stand on the box with you," he said. "I can try to pull out the nail."

"No, that won't work. You can't pull it out with your bare hands. It's driven too deeply into the wall. I need you to find me a hacksaw, Juanito."

"I know what that is."

"So do I," Pedro chimed in.

"Can you find one," Brognola said, "and bring it to me without anyone seeing you?"

Before either boy could answer, the floor creaked on the other side of the door. Then the door opened wide, revealing a big man with blond hair and hard, brown eyes. His chiseled features had ever so slightly gone to fat, a chin once perfectly square now had rounded edges. Still, he was athletic-looking, agile. He was dressed in a navy-blue jogging suit.

"What are you two doing in here?" Don Jorge Luis Samosa demanded of the children. "I told you to stay away from this room, to stay off this floor."

Juanito and Pedro looked at the tops of their sandals.

"Juanito, I want an answer."

The eight-year-old summoned his courage, looked up and said, "We were curious."

The drug lord started to smile, then caught himself.

Brognola was startled by the expression in the man's eyes. That Samosa would feel pride at the boy's truthfulness and bravery puzzled him.

"Is your curiosity satisfied?" Samosa asked.

Both boys nodded.

"I'm not going to punish you, this time," Samosa said. "But if you dare to disobey me again, you will regret it, I promise."

"Yes, sir," the children replied.

Brognola could see that Ortiz's boys were afraid of this man, but it wasn't the kind of terror he had expected. Juanito and Pedro weren't concerned about the physical danger they were in; they were afraid of losing Samosa's respect.

His affection.

The side-by-side resemblance confirmed what Brognola had suspected.

"What has Mr. Bennett done?" Juanito asked, using the alias Brognola had given him. "Why have you let Ramon hurt him?"

"He's the enemy," Samosa answered. "His mission in life is to take everything I have and see me dead. That's his crime and why he must be punished."

The boys turned their big brown eyes on Brognola. They looked confused and frightened.

"Breakfast is ready downstairs," the drug lord told them. "Let's see how quickly you can get down there. Scoot!" He clapped his hands together to get their attention and immediate compliance.

After Juanito and Pedro had raced out of the room, Samosa stepped closer to Brognola, who now knew why so much effort had been expended to take the boys from the San Diego safehouse, why their escape route had been so convoluted. He understood why their mother had risked and ultimately given up her own life to protect them from Don Jorge Samosa.

And he also knew that he couldn't count on Juanito and Pedro to help him get away.

"Those are two fine sons you have, there," Brognola said. "You and their mother must have been very proud of them. By the way, do they know their papa paid to have her killed?"

Samosa didn't answer the question. "I have some news to pass on that I'm sure will interest you," he said. "As you know, the first Mexican drug-interdiction vessel is scheduled to be launched in Mazatlán this morning. Your government has invested a lot of money to make it hard for me to continue to do business. But I always seem to find a way around obstacles, don't I? It's how I got where I am, on top of the heap. I know how to reinvest my profits...."

Brognola waited for the other shoe to drop.

And it did.

"The first ship is going to disappear shortly after its launch," Samosa said. "I have arranged for it to be sunk, scuttled in water too deep for it ever to be discovered or recovered, sending eighty million dollars in U.S. taxpayer contributions down the tubes."

"What's one wrecked ship going to get you?" Brognola said.

"Not just wrecked. Vanished without explanation. No debris, no survivors, no clues. We both know that the whole DIV program will be put on hold while the Mexican and American governments play the blame game back and forth. Respective panels of experts will duel over what happened and why for months, maybe years to come. In the meantime, I'll run my business as usual."

Though outwardly Brognola didn't react to this revelation, his insides were churning. The DIV program was the single most critical element of Stony Man's multipronged plan to bring down the Samosa cartel. If the state-of-the-art pursuit ships didn't get built, didn't actually go on patrol, none of the damage the Executioner had inflicted so far would have a lasting effect. Dead cartel soldiers could be easily replaced, along with the network of bribed government officials and the lost gold and cocaine. The only hope for real, permanent change in the criminal status quo was to strangle the smugglers' sea routes. If the prototype DIV went down, Samosa would win. It was as simple as that.

"This is your last day on earth, Fed," the Don said. "It'll take another twelve hours for Three Nails to finish with you, assuming he can keep his temper under wraps and do the job right. By the end of your journey of pain, you will have given up every person you know, betrayed every secret you possess. You and I know this for a fact."

Brognola glared at the drug lord, but said nothing. In the back of his mind something finally clicked.

The torture game was ninety-nine percent psychological. The other one percent was physical: the beating of the soles of the feet, the electrodes to the testicles, the spike driven through the palm of the hand. The shock of physical pain, the threat of more brutality to come, eventually convinced the victim that he was powerless and doomed. The victim, in effect, bought into the torturer's view of the situation. That all his training hadn't prepared him for what these animals had done to him, that he'd allowed Murillo and Samosa to get the psychological advantage made Brognola's blood boil.

"Ramon will rejoin you after breakfast," Samosa promised. "He believes that torture goes much more smoothly on a full stomach." With that, the drug lord left him.

The big Fed stared at the closed door without seeing it. The suicide card was no longer his to play. Samosa had inadvertently given him a reason to fight. His obligation, professional and personal, was to somehow get off the frigging wall and warn the Mexican navy before it was too late.

Gritting his teeth, Brognola let his knees buckle, let himself collapse, dropping all of his body weight on the spike, trying to break the bones in his hand and rip himself free. The pain made him see stars, and his shriek of agony filled the room.

No go.

On shaking legs, he raised himself, and tried again, harder.

This time, the pain sheared his consciousness like a falling ax blade, and he blacked out.

3

Eugenio Sanchez sat with the heels of his silver-toe-capped lizard-skin cowboy boots propped on the balcony rail. Beside his right hand, on the red gingham oilcloth covering the table, rested his third cup of black coffee and a loaded SIG-Sauer pistol. The morning was cool, with a refreshing hint of breeze. The heat wouldn't start to become oppressive for another hour or so. Above his head, around the hummingbird feeders that hung from the balcony rafters, iridescent little birds flitted back and forth, chirping as they battled for territory.

Sanchez's view from the balcony was of green-on-green low scrub-covered hills and a narrow road rising from the valley floor in the distance, as it snaked around the turns.

At the next table, Lucian and Pandro had their own side arms fieldstripped and neatly laid out on sheets of newspaper, and Tito, the youngest man on the team, heartily gulped down the remains of the second full breakfast he'd ordered. When it came to food, the rail-thin teenager from Oaxaca was a bottomless pit.

In the distance, Sanchez caught the sound of a car approaching.

The others heard it, too. Tito immediately dropped his fork onto his plate; Lucian and Pandro set down their cleaning rags. Sanchez pushed up from his chair and stepped behind a pair of huge binoculars mounted on a tripod alongside the balcony rail.

Moving from left to right, he tracked the car from viewpoint to viewpoint as it wound through the turns. It was a silver Nissan four-door sedan. From the angle he had, it looked like there was just one person in the vehicle.

"One man," he said to the others as he drew back from the lenses' rubber eyecups. "Car looks like an airport rental. Maybe a tourist..."

He pulled his walkie-talkie from its belt holster and informed the hacienda on the summit that a lone visitor was coming, probably a lost tourist, and that his team would deal with the driver if he stopped at the restaurant. If he didn't stop, the ball was in the court of the men guarding the road uphill from Sanchez's crew, between the restaurant and the hacienda.

As Sanchez replaced the walkie-talkie in its holster, Tito pushed the plate of *huevos rancheros* away without finishing and wiped his mouth with the back of his hand. Lucian and Pandro muttered curses as they hurriedly reassembled their pistols. The stranger's ETA was four minutes.

"Tito," Sanchez said, "go watch the parking lot. See if this guy drives by or stops."

The skinny gunman nodded, got up quickly and ran for the exit.

After what had happened to cartel forces elsewhere over the past few days, everybody, including Sanchez, was on edge. Many drug soldiers had died at the Murillo brothers' rancho in Baja California, and even more had been killed in Costa Rica. An unidentified enemy had dealt devastating blows to well-armed men in hard sites, and then vanished without a trace.

Was it a campaign by a rival cartel, perhaps the Colombians, to take over the Samosa smuggling routes? Or was the U.S. government behind the operation? There was much speculation among the drug soldiers, but no one knew the truth.

The fact that most of the dead guys had been Costa Ricans and Panamanians, and not Mexicans, was the only bright side as far as Sanchez was concerned. Based on his experience working for the cartel in Central America, he was of the opinion that Costa Ricans and Panamanians couldn't fight to save their own asses. Neither country had a standing army anymore.

He had been warned by the security bosses at the hacienda not to discount any potential threats. His observation crew had been ordered to treat a lone stranger with the same respect and caution as a platoon of marines in full battle gear. Sanchez didn't for a minute believe that one person could have done all the damage reported in Baja and Costa Rica. And he was confident that the four members of his team could take out one guy, no matter how fucking good he was. He and his men had earned many notches on their gun butts in the service of the cartel. They knew how to hunt and kill as a unit, and to kill quickly. And they sure as hell wouldn't be taken by surprise, which, in Sanchez's opinion, was the only way a lone gunman could ever hope to take out four guys.

Sanchez glanced over his shoulder, across the banquet room. Except for the few key employees necessary to keep the kitchen running and the forty or so Samosa gunmen in town well fed between guard shifts, the sprawling hillside restaurant was deserted. This was always the case when Don Jorge Luis Samosa was in residence at the hacienda in the village above.

A few years back, Samosa had bought up the entire town. He owned every building, every blade of grass. Every person was, directly or indirectly, on the cartel payroll. He had rescued the isolated hilltop hamlet from decades of poverty and neglect, and his infusion of cash had stopped its residents' migration to the coastal cities. When he visited the area, maybe four or five times year, he used the village as an operations center and hideout.

When Samosa was in town, the place was locked down by his private army of gunmen. The local police and the federal drug cops were well compensated to keep their distance from Corto de Vista, and to convince any and all outsiders they came across to do the same. When the Don wasn't in residence, life went on more normally. The children attended the four-room school he had built for them, farmers planted crops with seed and fertilizer he paid for, and craftspeople made knickknacks for the tourist trade in Mazatlán and trucked the goods there in vehicles he provided. None of them had to worry about surviving lean times. Drug money took care of their essentials.

The townsfolk who'd had a problem with the source of this good fortune had simply packed up and left. Most people stayed and gratefully took the charity. They welcomed the idea of having a patron to look after their basic needs. The current residents' ancestors had all worked for the man who'd founded the town. He was long dead now, and his family long bankrupt, which had left the villagers and their offspring to fend for themselves. They hadn't done well on their own.

Corto de Vista was never a tourist destination. It was too far from Mazatlán's big beach hotels and the curving hairpin of a road above the restaurant was too narrow for tour buses, so the only way visitors could get to the summit and the village center was by foot. The reward at the end of a forty-five-degree hill climb in brutal heat was hardly worth the effort. At the top there was a small town square with a tiny concrete and wrought-iron bandstand, an old stone church and, at the very summit, the hacienda built by the hamlet's founder in the 1850s. Prior to Samosa's takeover, Corto de Vista had tried to trade on its quaintness. As a kind of desperate last gasp, it became an art center. The front rooms of the little adobe houses on both sides of the square were turned into crafts galleries and showrooms.

It was a disaster. Too few visitors came, the folk art collected dust and moths ate holes in the yarn paintings and serapes.

A few tourists from Mazatlán still occasionally wandered up the road to the restaurant. When the drug lord was visiting, they were dissuaded from going any farther by men like Sanchez. Men with guns, and no patience.

Tito reappeared after a moment, a smirk on his long, thin face as he hurried across the room. Taking a seat at the table with Lucian and Pandro, he said, ''He's coming in, he's right behind me. One guy. A fucking gringo.''

When the driver of the silver Sentra stepped through the doorway, all eyes turned his way, sizing him up. He was tall, lean and dark-haired. He wore loose-fitting faded blue jeans and a new-looking black T-shirt with a full-color jumping sailfish across the chest. He had a black nylon backpack slung over his left shoulder. There were no weapons visible, not even a folding knife in a belt sheath.

Because of the wraparound sunglasses the guy had on, Sanchez couldn't see his eyes. He didn't like the way the stranger moved, though. He was way too relaxed, way too comfortable. Especially considering the fact that Lucian and Pandro had left their guns in plain sight and within easy reach on the table in front of them.

Without a word or a nod of greeting, the stranger walked over to a balcony table thirty feet away and took a seat facing them. His expression below the sunglasses was unreadable, virtually a blank canvas.

If this guy had something to do with the earlier attacks, Sanchez told himself, he had to be stone crazy to come walking in there all by himself. Either that or his showing up solo was some kind of diversionary tactic, a feint to distract them from the real danger elsewhere. Looking at the guy, so cool and detached, so in control, made Sanchez's trigger finger itch.

Aside from their observation-post duties, his team's job was to turn away potential sightseers. And that translated into anything from threatening stares to murder, whatever it took. In this case, the hard-stare treatment didn't seem to have any effect.

The stranger picked up a stained paper menu and began reading it.

Right on cue, the swinging doors to the kitchen opened and the restaurant's manager rushed over to where the newcomer sat.

Gringo on gringo, Sanchez thought, folding his arms across his chest.

Dressed in extra-tight jeans with a fancy tooled leather belt, a long-sleeved black satin cowboy shirt with mother-of-pearl snap buttons and custom-made cowboy boots, the manager of the Restaurante Corto de Vista looked every inch a Texan redneck. Joe Bob Cheever was a big man. The combination of barrel chest and slender legs made him look top-heavy and always a little off balance. Cheever was a notorious bullshit artist and drunk. Though he started in on the tequila when he first rolled out of bed, he didn't start showing the booze until much later in the day. By five p.m. he was chewing out the help, maybe slapping some of the women around, if he could catch them.

Cheever had spent several years trying to make a go of the restaurant before Samosa had bought up the town. Once the Texan had been top man in Corto de Vista, king of the hill, ordering everybody around like he was God, even though the restaurant's revival had failed miserably. Now he was nobody. Less than nobody. Cheever glanced over at Sanchez as he approached the stranger's table, awaiting instructions, like a good little bootlicker.

Sanchez shook his head.

"I'm sorry, pal," Cheever drawled in a gravelly, chain-smoker's voice, "but the kitchen's closed."

"Can I get some coffee?" the tall man asked.

"We just ran out."

The stranger took off the sunglasses. His eyes were an unusual color: ice-blue. He seemed not to notice the group of armed men ten yards away, glaring at him. "That's too bad," he said. "Does your rest room work? I'd sure like to relieve myself before I start driving back."

"It's downstairs. Just follow the signs, pal."

The big guy thanked him, got up, slipped his pack over his shoulder and headed for the lavatory.

Sanchez waited until he was out of sight around a corner, then picked up his SIG and rose from his chair. He gestured for the others to follow him. The butterflies skittering in his stomach were a good thing, he assured himself. They meant he was on his toes.

The warnings of his superiors and recent disasters aside, Sanchez was pleased that something interesting had come along to break the morning's usual, dull routine. He and his boys were about to make the gringo tourist vanish. His rental car would likewise disappear. The jungle was a great place to hide things, permanently. All you needed was a machete to clear a path through the brush and a shovel to make the hole. Sanchez didn't like digging graves because of the way it beat up his hands and scuffed his lizard-skin boots.

Digging graves was what Lucian, Pandro and Tito were there for.

As he approached the corner, he raised the SIG in a two-handed grip.

THE EXECUTIONER had examined the four Hispanic thugs who had faced him. They were a standard-issue, cartel hit crew, all dressed in shiny polyester gray-and-black short-sleeve knit shirts, baggy black slacks and silver-decorated Mexi-pimp cowboy boots. None of them wore body armor. They were used to having their way without getting their snappy clothes messed up.

And without taking return fire.

The leader, thirtyish, with black hair raked straight back from an exceptionally low and greasy forehead, didn't look particularly quick of hand or feet. Or brain, for that matter. Under the squinty-eyed, bared-teeth, I'd-love-to-kill-you mask, he was clearly uneasy. Maybe he wasn't used to having his best hard look ignored.

The lack of fear or anger or aggressive intent on Bolan's face accurately reflected his mental state at that moment. He was emotionally detached from the situation, but not indifferent to it. Under total control. In the face of impending violence, he was frighteningly calm. Focused. The Executioner was in a zone all his own.

The kill zone.

Few if any men had been where he'd been, or done what he'd done. In the name of justice, Mack Bolan had filled cemeteries by the dozens, row upon row of white marble tombstones stretching to the horizon. Under the markers were the rotting corpses of men who deserved to die: mafiosi, terrorists, mass murderers. Bolan's war without end, begun so long ago, had taught him the limits of his own reactions, his instincts, his marksmanship, his striking power and his will to survive. It had also taught him to read the limitations of others at a glance.

The Mexicans who sat thirty feet away were dead men breathing.

As for the drawling cowboy, the maître d' or whatever

the hell he was, unless he got in the way or did something way out of character, he wasn't a target.

When Bolan got up from the table and started following the signs to the bathroom, he knew the hit crew would come after him. He was counting on it. If things had been different, if Brognola's life and the security of Stony Man Farm hadn't hung in the balance, he would have picked a less direct plan of attack. If he'd had all day to get the job done, he'd have avoided the road and the restaurant altogether and used the jungle for cover while he worked himself into a high-ground position with a long gun. From a sniper's hide overlooking the village, he could have softened up the enemy, reducing the odds without exposing himself, then penetrated the defensive perimeter of the hacienda, where his controllers believed Brognola was being held.

In the best of all possible worlds, the Executioner would have chosen a less risky plan. In the real world, he had to lower his head, grit his teeth and, based on the satellite recon surveillance of the village's topography and infrastructure, go for it. A straight-line, no-prisoners route up the road meant he couldn't detour around the four Mexicans. He had to deal with them now, because if he didn't they could warn the guard posts up the hill. They could also come at his back when he was otherwise occupied. And they could make his retreat with Brognola difficult, or even impossible. It was just a question of choosing the right killing field. Someplace cozy, out of sight and earshot.

The bathroom signs led him down four flights of concrete stairs to the lowest floor of the building. The bottom level had suffered noticeably more wear and tear than the upper stories. The view from each of the floors opened onto a full-length balcony. Close to the railings it was pleasant and airy. Away from the balconies, the banquet rooms were dark, with low ceilings and dim, artificial lighting. The connecting hallways were even dimmer. The effect was cavelike.

Bolan turned down a long hallway. A series of windows on the left-hand wall looked onto the restaurant's bakery, where a couple of extremely short Mexican women in white uniforms were making enough pies to feed a small army. Banana cream, from the look of it. They smiled shyly at him as he passed.

He was trying hard not to think about Brognola, about the real possibility that when he reached the end of the line, he wouldn't find his old friend alive. It was probable that he wouldn't find a corpse, either.

Ahead, another corridor crossed this one. A sign on the wall indicated a right turn to the bathroom. When Bolan rounded the corner, he looked down a much narrower hallway. At the far end was a small balcony. Beside a doorway on the floor along the right-hand wall was a big yellow plastic bucket with a mop stuck in it. Beside the bucket was a small yellow easel signboard. On one side, in Spanish, it read, Closed for Cleaning; on the other, Out of Order. There was no lavatory attendant in sight.

Bolan tried the door marked *Hombres*. It opened into a dark room. He found the light switch, which was connected to a single weak bulb over the mirror. The bathroom had three stalls and a sink. There were no windows. As he closed the door behind him, he saw that the knob had a tab lock on the inside. He left the door unlocked and quickly checked the stalls, which were empty.

It would do, he decided.

It was far enough away from the dining rooms to hide the sounds of a scuffle, even gunshots. And it had a door that could be locked from the inside to conceal the corpses and postpone their discovery.

Bolan took the sound suppressed Beretta 93-R from his

pack and tapped the bulb with its muzzle, shattering it with a soft pop and hiss, and plunging the room in darkness.

A second or two passed while his eyes acclimated.

Then he heard muttered voices from the hallway and heavy footsteps outside.

Dead men walking.

4

Before Eugenio Sanchez reached the corner, Joe Bob Cheever stepped in front of him, a grim expression on his face. "You're not planning on killing him in the bathroom, I hope," he said.

Sanchez lowered his weapon reluctantly. "What do you care where we do the job?"

"Take him outside, for Christ's sake," the Texan said. "If you shoot him in the bathroom, it'll make a terrible mess."

Sanchez stared up at Cheever for a long moment, then he said, "You're a fussy man, *señor*," which translated into, "You're more a woman than a man, *señor*."

The other soldiers sniggered.

Cheever's face turned red.

"Maybe you'd better stay out of the way," Sanchez suggested. "Otherwise, you might get hit by something nasty."

The Texan stiffened, but he took heed of the warning. He clunked off in his cowboy boots, muttering to himself.

"Idiot!" Sanchez spit, as he racked the slide on his SIG. Then to the others he said, "Come on, let's get the fucker."

The gringo stranger took some catching, as it turned out. Even though Sanchez and the hit crew broke into a jog, they couldn't overtake him before he made it to the washroom.

The crew closed in on the bathroom door, four automatic pistols covering it as they approached. Sanchez stepped over the bucket and mop, and put his back to the wall beside the door.

"We take no chances with this guy," he said very softly. "I'll handle backup. You three go in. Lucian and Tito low, Pandro high. Whatever moves in there, shoot it all to hell."

The three gunners didn't seem to care that they were getting the ugly end of the stick. In fact, they were smiling. The bravado was a front. Sanchez knew because he'd been there, done that. To complain about the danger he was putting them in would have cost them face. And face was everything to these guys. If you wanted to climb the ladder of power, you had to be hard as iron.

"When I turn the knob, kick open the door," Sanchez whispered to Lucian.

THE EXECUTIONER backed into the farthest stall from the door and took a seat on the commode. He held the stall's door open with a knee, set the 93-R's fire selector for tri-burst, and folded down the skeleton front grip. The forward grip was necessary to control the muzzle climb of burst mode. After dropping the safety catch, he braced the Beretta in a two-handed grip against the edge of the door.

His first shot would give away his position, so it had to be in the ten ring. He didn't want answering fire in the enclosed space. Jacketed Parabellums would cut the thin sheet metal of the stalls like tissue paper.

He had time enough to slow his breathing before the red dance started. With a resounding thud, a boot drove the door inward. The accompanying rush of wind carried the smell of aftershave. Baggy pants rustled as three dimly backlit forms moved through the doorway, two low, one high. A fourth head remained outside, in the hall.

Bolan's trigger finger was already bearing down. The pistol bucked between his fists, stuttering softly in triplicate. The low-powered subsonic rounds had just enough blow back to cycle the pistol's action. They made it much easier to hold steady on a target. In the darkness, Parabellum rounds slapped flesh.

The man diving low to the left let out a groan. Unable to stop himself, he crashed into the sink and slipped facedown to the floor.

The Executioner swung his sights to the right, firing through the next target, the man moving upright. As the 93-R triple-timed, he got a glimpse of arms opening wide and a body being jolted backward, folding like a lawn chair as his knees buckled.

The close quarters of the bathroom made the stench of blood and reflexively voided bowels suddenly overwhelming.

Sensing his own looming fate, the third man pivoted, stood and tried to reverse course.

Bolan held the Beretta steady and tightened on the trigger. Three 9 mm bullets caught the thug beneath the right shoulder blade. The tightly spaced slugs up-angled through his chest, shredding his heart. Dead on his feet, the gunner's forward momentum carried him straight into the wall beside the open door. His forehead hit with a solid *thunk*. He slid down the wall and collapsed on the floor.

Before the Executioner could make it a clean sweep, the head of the fourth shooter ducked back around the doorjamb.

Bolan lunged out of the stall. Reaching the doorway, he saw the man running away from him, toward the balcony. Framed by the bright light ahead, he was trying to speak into the walkie-talkie in his right hand as he ran.

The Executioner released several shots from an unbraced hold. The muzzle climb spread the impact points of the Parabellums up the man's back, from the base of his spine to the base of his neck. He crashed to the floor on his face. The walkie-talkie slipped from his hand and skittered twenty feet toward the balcony.

Bolan ran to the still-kicking body, grabbed hold of the collar of the man's knit shirt and, before the blood really started gushing, hauled him across the polished tile floor to the little balcony. A second later, he sent him tumbling headfirst over the rail. The dying man cartwheeled into the dense brush some fifty feet below.

Returning to the bathroom, the Executioner checked the other bodies for signs of life. Finding none, he stepped back out into the hall, turned the doorknob's lock and shut the door. After putting the Beretta back in his pack, he moved the yellow Out of Order sign in front of the doorway.

It would buy him all the time he needed.

Heading back down the hall the way he'd come, he carried the black backpack in one hand. The other hand was thrust through the open zipper, fingers around the grip of the 93-R.

To get back to the parking lot and the rental car he'd left there, Bolan had to walk by the cash register. As he did, the maître d' popped out of an open doorway of the office behind it. The man's mouth dropped when he saw who it was. He wasn't expecting to see him again, at least not in this life. Right away, he lunged forward and started to make a grab for something below the counter.

"Don't do that," Bolan warned him. He raised the concealed 93-R to head height.

The Texan stared at the hand in the pack and the way it was being pointed at his face. "Jesus, have you got a gun in there?" he said, raising his hands in the air. "What do you want? Money? The till is right there. There isn't much, but help yourself, take it all."

Snapping a cap on the guy would have been the simplest solution to the security problem he presented. Bolan could have easily hidden his body in the office. But the cowboy seemed like the restaurant's boss man, which meant somebody might miss him and come looking for him. Besides, Bolan saw a need the guy could fill. To cover the most ground in the shortest time, a tour guide would come in handy.

"You lived around here long?" he asked.

"Huh? Yeah, nine years."

"Great," Bolan said. "You're coming with me. Step out from behind the counter."

The Texan suddenly looked very tired and very scared. As he rounded the counter, he said, "What do you want from me?"

"We'll talk about that in the parking lot," the Executioner told him. "Lower your hands and walk in front of me. If anybody asks where you're going, just say you're stepping outside for some air."

Bolan quick-marched the guy right up to the rear bumper of the Sentra. "Step aside and put your hands flat on the fender," he said.

When the Texan had done what he'd been told, Bolan unlocked and popped the trunk.

His captive eyed the compartment with dread. "Jesus, you're not going to make me get in there, are you? I don't like closed spaces."

The Executioner reached inside and lifted out a heavy, black ballistic-nylon duffle bag and slung it over his shoulder. "We're walking, not driving," he told the guy.

From the pained expression on his face, Bolan knew that the cowboy had guessed what was in the duffle: more and bigger weapons.

"Who the hell are you?" he said.

"That's not important."

"Who sent you?" the guy went on. "Was it the Colombians? Are you here to make a hit on the Don?"

The Executioner didn't answer.

It was his first confirmation that the drug lord Samosa might actually be present inside the hilltop KZ. That would be the icing on the cake.

"I want to go up to the village," he told his prisoner. "I don't want to be seen by the guys guarding the road. I need you to point out their positions, so stay nice and calm and quiet, no matter what happens."

"If I do that, if I do everything you want, will you let me live?"

"If you don't do what I say, you'll be the next to die."

"Fuck!" the guy said. He closed his eyes and shook his head. "I should have seen this coming. I should have left this place years ago, when I had the chance. Man, do I ever need a drink."

"Let's go."

They crossed the gravel lot to the edge of the road. To the right, it rose steeply, winding between small buildings on both sides. The houses and shops were shuttered up tight. Nobody was home. The road curved out of sight around a flank of the hill seventy-five yards ahead.

The cowboy led him across the road and the drainage ditch on the other side. Beating through brush and vines, he located the start of what looked like a game trail, about a foot wide. The two of them started trudging up the grade. The going got very steep before they topped the ridge.

Bolan's conscripted guide bent over, face red, hands on knees, gasping for breath. "Need to rest a second, please," he said.

The Executioner let him suck air while he took in the scenery on the far side of the hill. Peeking out of the scrub jungle here and there, perched on the opposite slopes were little huts with steeply pitched, thatched palm roofs and mud walls. Unlike the houses along the main road, they looked occupied: laundry hung from lines strung between palm trees. He could see small gardens, chicken coops and fruit trees clinging to the hillside.

"Where's the first roadblock?" he asked his prisoner.

The guy straightened, still wheezing a little. He pointed to the road below them, where it made an extreme hairpin turn. "Down there," the Texan said. "That's it."

A tall, narrow, yellow-beige house stood at the point of the turn, its back side sloping up the hill. On the other side of the street, a maroon van and a brown-and-white Bronco were stopped on the skinny shoulder, their noses pointed downhill, their passenger sides facing Bolan. The van was half a car length in front of the SUV's front bumper, positioned so both vehicles could swerve out and seal off the road.

"How many guns?"

"Usually five or six."

The Executioner took a pair of compact Steiner binoculars from the backpack and scanned downrange. Because his angle of view was so steep, he couldn't see into either of the vehicles to do a target count. The windows of the van and the SUV were all rolled down.

"Can we get down to road level without being seen?" he said to the cowboy.

"We?"

"I don't like to repeat myself."

"Yeah, I think so...." the man said.

"Then, let's do it."

With the sweat-drenched Texan in the lead, they descended the steep slope behind the house, carefully working their way under the cover of the dense brush. The house had been built into the hillside. Its rear was one-story, while the road-facing side was three stories. It had a flat, corrugated sheet metal roof. Its exterior was concrete block, stuccoed over. At the back was a peeling, blue wooden door, and a single window.

"Anybody live here?" Bolan said as he peered through the dirty glass.

"Not when Samosa's in town," the Texan said. "Most of the people on the main road take a vacation when he's around, to get out of the way of the guards. They make it uncomfortable."

The blue door had a padlock on it. Bolan took a small pry bar from his pack and wrenched the hasp from the frame. He pushed the door inward. Inside, it was dark, airless and swelteringly hot.

They moved through the tiny first room, then started down a flight of steep, narrow stairs. The bottom floor of the house looked stripped. There were only a couple of pieces of furniture: a battered foam-leaking sofa and a kitchen table the size of a TV tray. In the front room, someone had nailed up orange plastic shopping bags for curtains on the dusty windows.

Bolan made the cowboy sit cross-legged on the floor while he took a look out at the street.

From this angle, he could see into both vehicles. There were two guys in the van's front seats, three more in the Bronco. The guys in the Bronco carried M-16s. They had the rifle butts resting beside them on the seats, the muzzles pointed out the windows.

"How much are the Colombians paying you, pal?" the cowboy asked him. "Whatever it is, you're not going to live to spend it. There are too many cartel soldiers out there and it gets a whole lot worse in the village. Samosa's got a goddamned army up there."

Bolan took a pair of handcuffs from the pack and secured the man's right wrist to his opposite ankle, leaving him a hand and leg free. "I need you to be real quiet for a few minutes," he said.

The prisoner didn't have to be told twice.

The Executioner opened the duffle and started pulling out his battle gear. He shrugged into a black ballistic-nylon combat harness, already fully loaded with its normal complement of frag and stun grenades, pouches stuffed with extra magazines for his autopistol, and a double-edged SOG Pentagon dagger hanging handle down in an inverted harness-strap sheath. He took the 93-R from his pack, unscrewed its suppressor and holstered the weapon in his harness.

From the duffle, he removed a pair of soft-sided zipper cases that held mini-Uzis. The SMG sound suppressors and a handful of 30-round stick magazines had been taped together in pairs, side to side, one facing throat up, the other down.

Bolan threaded the suppressors, then fitted the mags to the Uzi butts and slapped them home. After charging the cocking handles and slipping their nylon lanyards over his neck, he rolled on a pair of skintight black leather gloves.

"Nice and quiet, now, until I get back."

The cowboy nodded.

When Bolan tried the front door, it wouldn't open more than a quarter inch. There was another padlock on the far side. Abandoning the door, he opened a side window and slipped out of the house, creeping along the exterior wall to the corner of the building.

Staying well back from the edge, he pulled a small mirror with a flexible handle from his harness and used it to take a quick look around the bend. Inside the vehicles, all he saw were the backs of the soldiers' heads. The attention of the roadblock crew was momentarily focused on something in the opposite direction.

The Executioner came around the corner at a dead run, the mini-Uzis up and ready in both fists. Six long strides took him almost all the way across the road before the man in the back seat of the Bronco saw him. The guy's eyes got huge and his mouth opened.

Before the drug soldier could shout a warning to his compadres, Bolan cut loose with both submachine guns, still charging the vehicles.

It wasn't fine work.

It was close and rough.

With his right hand, he stitched craters up the passenger's door of the van and through the open window. For a fraction of a second, the passenger shuddered under the hail of bullet impacts. Then his head exploded in a puff of pink, bathing the inner surface of the windshield in liquified brains.

As Bolan was doing his best not to break glass in order to keep the noise down, he didn't shoot through the windshield of the Bronco. He took another two strides, so he could angle his fire through the open passenger windows, front and rear. As the gunmen inside tried desperately to get their rifles out the SUV's windows and aimed at him, he pinned the trigger of the Uzi in his left hand, streaming bullets into the vehicle, clipping hunks out of the two drug soldiers on the passenger side, as well as the front headrest and the doorpost.

Under the hail of full-auto gunfire, the Bronco's rear door swung open, and a man slid out, first to his knees, then onto his face, stone dead but gripping his assault rifle in both hands.

The van's nearly headless passenger slipped from view, revealing the ashen-faced driver who had been protected from the initial burst by the other guy's body. The Executioner poured 9 mm rounds through the window, making the guy behind the wheel twist and shake; the savage, multiple hits buffeted him against the inside of the door. Then the Uzi's action locked back, mag empty.

The driver of the Bronco was likewise untouched. And

he had sense enough to forget about returning fire, to open his door and make a dash for the cover of the hillside jungle.

Good idea.

But it came a little late.

Bolan shoved the Uzi in his left hand through the Bronco's passenger's window, and fired through it and out the open door on the other side, hitting the running driver in the middle of the back. The nearly simultaneous rounds lifted the guy off his feet and sent him flying headfirst into the bush. Then the second Uzi locked back as well.

The Executioner let that weapon drop inside the Bronco, onto the dead passenger's lap. Then he dumped the other SMG's magazine onto his palm. He flipped it around and jammed the fully loaded spare into the butt. As he snapped the actuator, chambering the first round in the stack, the hinged side doors of the van swung open and two guys he'd missed bailed out.

One had a sawed-off 12-gauge shotgun, the other had an M-16 rifle.

From a distance of ten feet, the Executioner poured withering fire into the chests of the two gunmen, emptying the fresh mag. Neither one managed to get off a shot before they were blown to pieces.

That made seven down.

Bolan retrieved the other Uzi and quickly reloaded it. Then he checked inside the van. Finding it clear, he hauled three of the bodies into the cargo compartment and shut the doors. The man feebly kicking in the bushes he left alone.

Reaching into the van, he gripped the driver's hair and pulled his body off the steering wheel. He propped the fresh corpse against the door in as natural a pose as possible. There was nothing he could do about the inside of the windshield, which dripped pink slime.

That done, he moved on to the Bronco. He dragged the dead passenger across the console and into the driver's seat, then used the seat belt to lash the guy in place.

It wasn't great, but it would have to do.

The Executioner crossed the street. When he climbed back through the window, he caught his tour guide pouring tequila from a half-pint glass down his throat with his uncuffed hand.

"Better save some of that for later," Bolan said.

"I might be dead later," the Texan countered, but he lowered the bottle anyway.

"Where's the next roadblock?" Bolan asked as he unlocked and removed the handcuffs.

"It's in front of the schoolhouse. You can't see it from here. It's uphill, around the next bend."

The Executioner tossed one of the mini-Uzis on the floor. He replaced the twin mag in the other and rehung the weapon around his neck. Kneeling, he drew a foam-lined long-gun case from the duffle. He unzipped it and quickly assembled the two sections of an Accurized Colt M-16, scoped with a Trijicon advanced combat optical gun sight. He screwed on the short-range sniper rifle's sound suppressor and checked the 30-round magazine to make sure it was full. Then he slipped a double handful of extra mags into the backpack and slung it over his shoulder.

"We're going out that window," he told the Texan. "Stay close behind me."

When they were around the front of the house, Bolan trotted up the road a little ways, with the cowboy right on his heels. He slowed as the street's bend came into view on the right. Moving to the corner of the next house, he used his binoculars to study the kill zone up the hill.

On the other side of the hill's flank was a one-story flat-roofed building. Its concrete walls had been painted a cheery mulberry color. Only about a third of the schoolhouse was visible from where Bolan stood. The high, narrow, horizontal windows that faced him were decorated with brightly colored pictures of birds. Above the windows, shading them and the front of the building, was a metal awning. Rimming the edge of the road was a waist-high concrete-block planter. The planter didn't have any flowers growing in it, but Bolan could see a man's bald head sticking up from the other side. Behind the seated man was the top of the schoolhouse's front door.

The Executioner turned to his guide and said, "This won't do. I can't see the whole layout from here. And we can't go any farther up the road without being seen ourselves."

The Texan didn't say anything.

"I need some elevation," Bolan told him. Then he gave the guy a shove back the way they'd come.

A couple of minutes later, the Executioner and the cowboy had hauled themselves up onto the roof of the house they'd broken into. Bolan crab-crawled to the peak and looked over.

From this height, he had a much better view. He could see three gunmen sitting on folding chairs in the shaded walkway between the road and the school's front wall. The concrete planter blocked all but their heads and shoulders from gunfire. Their assault rifles were leaning against the building behind them, within easy reach.

The sound of music drifted over to them. Faint, but recognizable. It was the "Mexican Hat Dance," played very badly on accordion and violin.

"Are there kids in there?" Bolan demanded.

The cowboy shrugged. "There could be some in the playground behind the building, I suppose. It's hard to say. The school's closed on account of Samosa being here. Folks who haven't gone to visit out-of-town relatives usually keep their kids inside their own yards."

When Bolan looked back, he got the straight answer to his question. Through the binoculars, he saw a girl of maybe ten, in a pink dress, peek out around the school's front door.

One of the thugs turned and said something to her, the others laughed, and she ducked back inside, slamming the door.

Things had just gotten a little more complicated.

The Executioner put down the binoculars and picked up the Colt M-16.

5

Hacienda Corto de Vista

Juanito gave his little brother a kick under the table. When Pedro looked up, a shocked and hurt expression on his face, Juanito nodded at the big heap of papaya slices still sitting on the younger boy's plate.

Their father wouldn't excuse them from breakfast until they'd eaten every bite. Those were the rules.

Pedro stabbed a piece of fruit with his fork and wedged it into his mouth. He chewed and swallowed as fast as he could, then stabbed another slice.

The adults sitting around the table weren't paying any attention to the boys. Their father was talking about the helicopter trip they were about to take. Ramon Murillo was going to stay behind to look after things.

"I don't want you doing any more damage to our friend, the Fed, while I'm gone," Samosa said. "He has important information that I want. Do you understand?"

Ramon Murillo nodded and smiled obediently, but his black eyes glittered in a scary way.

Juanito stared down at his clean plate. He could hardly bring himself to look at Murillo. The man terrified him. And he was positive that no matter what his papa said, Murillo was going to follow his own black heart.

Pedro was slowing down on the papaya. He looked disgusted.

Juanito kicked him again and mimed the words: "Eat! Eat!"

Little Pedro speared the last slice.

The boys were supposed to go with their father to see some new ship he had bought. They were going to leave soon. Juanito would have been excited about the helicopter ride, but he couldn't stop thinking about Mr. Bennett up in the attic room, with a big nail through his hand that pinned him to the wall.

Juanito's papa had taught him to be self-reliant. He had spared no expense to nurture that quality. His mother, Yovana, had taught him a sense of right and wrong. The boy walked a tightrope, strung across a deep crevasse. Should he obey his father, who he worshipped? Or should he come to the aid of a person who had risked his life to protect him and his brother?

Pedro carefully set his fork down beside his empty plate. He wiped the juice from around his mouth with his napkin.

"May we be excused, Papa?" Juanito asked.

"Yes, you can go," Samosa said. He added, "Don't wander too far. I don't want to have to send a search party out for you two. We're leaving in ten minutes."

Juanito and Pedro hurried out of the dining room. The hacienda was cool and dark, with very thick adobe walls painted a burnt pumpkin color and polished black marble floors. It was full of old junk their papa had brought in, stuff they weren't supposed to play with. There were many men with guns, just standing around the corridors, looking bored, like they always did.

"Where are we going?" Pedro asked, breaking into a run to keep up with his brother.

"Just come on and stop whining."

Juanito led him to a doorway that opened onto a rear courtyard inside the compound's high walls. Bright sunlight washed banks of flowers. A big circular tile fountain gurgled and splashed. In the far corner of the garden was a small brick shed, where the landscape workers kept all their tools.

The minute Pedro saw where they were headed, he knew what his brother was up to. "I'm afraid," he said, grabbing hold of Juanito's arm and giving it a tug. "Papa will be very mad."

"Do you like Mr. Bennett?" Juanito asked him.

"Yes, he's a nice man. He tried to help us when there was all that shooting."

"Do you remember what Ramon did to the body-guard?"

Pedro clammed up. He refused to look his brother in the eye.

"In the bedroom," Juanito prompted, pushing him on the shoulder. "What he did in the bedroom. We weren't supposed to see what happened in there. Ramon's men put blankets over our heads to keep us from seeing as they took us out, but you and I peeked anyway. We *both* peeked."

Juanito shuddered as he recalled the halo of sprayed blood around the man's battered head, his body suspended from the wall from three huge nails driven through the palms of his hands and the top of his bare feet. There was a horrible smell.

"I remember."

"Well, Mr. Bennett will end up just like that unless we do something."

"But Papa—"

"First of all," Juanito said, as he opened the door of the shed, "if we hurry he'll never find out. Second, even if he does find out, what do you think he'll do to us?"

"Kill us?"

"Don't be stupid. He's not going to do that. He loves us."

Juanito stepped inside and immediately started rummaging through the tools in wooden crates on the shed's shelves.

Pedro came in, too, and started looking on the lower shelves. "Here's one," he said, almost at once. He held up a full-sized hacksaw with a rubber pistol grip and a big bow.

"Wrong kind," Juanito told him. "How am I going to hide something like that under my shirt?"

Pedro tossed it back in the box.

"This is what we need," Juanito said, snatching up a different style of tool. The short hacksaw blade was set in a knife-style handle, with a side support instead of a bow.

"Is it sharp?" Pedro asked.

Juanito tested it with his thumb. "Sharp enough. Let's go." He stuck the mini-hacksaw into the back pocket of his shorts, then pulled his T-shirt down over it.

"We never lied to Papa before, you know," Pedro said as they walked away from the shed.

"I know."

"If he asks us if we helped Mr. Bennett, are we going to tell him the truth?"

"What do you think?"

"I think I have to go to the bathroom."

"It can wait."

"Juanito, if Mr. Bennett gets away, he could hurt Papa. That's what Papa said."

"Papa is too strong and too smart for that," Juanito countered. "He's the strongest, smartest man alive."

6

Bolan flipped up the Trijicon scope's lens cap and positioned the M-16's butt. He didn't like the idea of using a schoolhouse with kids in it as a backstop for 5.56 mm rounds, but he had no choice. There wasn't time to go around the guard post. He had to go through it. He had to crush it.

With the sun slanting down over his right shoulder, there was no telltale downrange flare off the exposed lens. The Executioner scanned the low building more carefully. The shooting backstop was made of concrete blocks. Because the rounds in the suppressed M-16 were low-powered subsonics, the chances of a bullet going into the schoolhouse were very slight, even if they hit nothing in between. If his shots were on the money, the flesh and bone of his targets would slow the bullets enough so the concrete wall would stop them cold.

He considered putting a shot through one of the high windows, figuring that it would make the innocent people inside hit the dirt and stay there. It was a way to protect them, but it put him at a disadvantage having to waste his first shot and giving the opposition a chance to reach their guns. And there was the risk of the kids getting hit by flying glass.

Bolan decided there would be no preliminaries.

Through the scope he could see the drug soldiers enjoying the cool of the morning. The bald guy lighted up a fat cigar, leaned back in his chair and blew smoke rings into the air.

The Executioner turned the M-16's fire-control switch to single shot. The lens was sighted for a hundred yards. As he was about half that distance away, he used the scope's Mildot reticle to compensate for the range and angle, holding the aim point low. Then he practiced swinging the short weapon through the entire kill arc, hesitating a fraction of a second as he locked the sights on each target in turn.

Bang.

Bang.

Bang.

After taking another quick look at the closed front door and the corners of the building, he exhaled, touching the trigger with his finger's most sensitive spot, the center of the pad. He held the Mildot on the bald man's throat and squeezed.

The M-16 coughed and bucked weakly, spitting out a single shell. The recoil was so soft that Bolan never really lost his sight picture. He saw the bald guy bowled off his folding chair, vanishing behind the planter.

The drug soldier sitting next to him turned his head to look, unsure exactly what had happened.

Bolan was already taking up the trigger slack on his second shot. The M-16 let out another muffled report.

Through the Trijicon, sunlight glistened on a puff of red where the top of the man's head had been. He, too, dropped out of sight behind the planter.

The last guy on duty knew what was coming, but he couldn't do anything about it. It was like his butt was welded to the seat of the chair. Only his lips moved. If any sounds came out, Bolan couldn't hear them over the cough of the third shot.

The expression of shock and terror on the man's face

was obliterated as his worst fears came true, as a 5.56 mm tumbler roared through his skull.

Suddenly, there were no heads above the planter.

But there were brains on the schoolhouse wall behind.

"That's it?" the Texan said in amazement from behind him. "Three men, three shots?"

Bolan didn't answer. He scanned the KZ to make sure no more cartel soldiers were around. In his view field he saw the school's front door open. A woman with black hair peeked out. Seeing the dead men on the ground, she started screaming.

She was very loud.

The Executioner backed away from the peak of the roof and pulled a satellite recon photo from his harness. He unfolded it and showed it to the cowboy. "My map says there's a straightaway grade around the next bend that leads up to the town center."

"That's right."

"Where are the men in the square?"

"They move around. They've got Chevy Suburbans." He pointed at the streets on both sides of the square, then said, "All of the tourist shops are closed, locked up tight."

"How many guns are outside the hacienda?"

"Fifteen to twenty."

Up the road, the woman was still yelling for help. From the sound of it, she had enlisted a couple of kids to join in to boost the volume.

Sometime soon someone was going to get curious.

It required a change of plans.

"Get off the roof," Bolan told his captive. "Go on, hurry."

They crossed the road to the Bronco on a dead run. The Executioner opened the passenger's door and made the cowboy get in. He didn't want to sit in the bloody bucket, but one look at the corpse strapped into the other seat, and he did as he was told. Bolan used the handcuffs to lock the guy's wrists together above his head. He shut the passenger's door and moved to the driver's side of the SUV. Using his SOG knife, he cut the corpse free of the seat belt, dragged the body off the seat and dumped it onto the ground. Then Bolan got behind the wheel and cranked the engine.

As he cut a squealing U-turn and headed up the hill toward the waiting guns, the Texan swallowed hard and said, "This isn't a smart thing to do, pal. Not smart at all."

"Shut up," Bolan said.

7

Hal Brognola drifted through a dark, warm place where there was no pain, no threat and no fear; a place where he was free and safe. He would have stayed there much longer and been content, if a high-pitched voice hadn't kept bugging him to come back to the real world.

"Mister, mister, wake up," the piping voice said. "You've got to wake up, right now."

When the owner of the voice started shaking him by the arm, Brognola could no longer ignore it. He opened his eyes and was surprised to see Ortiz's boys standing beside him, looking very anxious.

Juanito reached behind his back and pulled something from under his T-shirt. "We brought you the saw," he said. "You've got to hurry. They'll be coming back in a minute."

Brognola took the minihacksaw from him. There wasn't time to ask the boys why they were taking such a risk. There was only time to be grateful. "Thank you both," he said. "I won't forget this, ever. Now, get out of here, quickly. Go!"

The boys ran out, closing the door after them.

Brognola set to work at once. He flattened the top of his forearm against the wall, straightening his fingers out of the way to expose the case-hardened nail's broad head. He rested the teeth of the saw on the shaft three-eighths of an inch in diameter, just behind the head, and began to cut in short, quick strokes. The sawing made a shrill racket, but there was nothing he could do about that. Once he got through the finish, the cutting went faster. Through his palm, he could feel the nail heating from the friction.

"Come on, come on," he muttered as sweat popped out on his forehead.

Then the nail head dropped to the floor, clattering, a tarnished nickel rolling to a stop a yard or so from the box on which he stood.

He was about to jerk his hand free when he heard approaching footsteps outside. The doorknob began to turn. There was no time to reach the door. He stuffed the saw into the left pocket of his trousers and closed his right hand over the broken spike, hiding it from view.

The door opened and Ramon Murillo stepped in. He was by himself, and he was carrying a framing hammer.

"Where's your backup?" Brognola said.

"I don't need any help to finish the job," Murillo snapped. "A man stuck to a wall by his hand is like an old woman, a crippled old woman. I can do anything to you that I want, whenever I want. This is the part I like the best."

As Murillo moved closer, Brognola fought the urge to look down at the severed nail head. The Mexican didn't seem to notice it or, if he did, he didn't pay any attention to it. He had other things on his mind.

"We have had no word from my brother, Roberto," he said. "Not since the attack on the drug stockpile. If he was still alive, he would have found a way to contact me by now."

The big Fed said nothing.

"It would have gone better for you if my brother Roberto was here. He was my conscience."

The idea that either of the Murillos knew what a conscience was made Brognola want to laugh, but he didn't.

"Roberto had all the brains," Murillo went on. "He could plan things. If it hadn't been for him, there never would have been a Murillo organization. Nobody in our family ever made it big, except us. Our mama was murdered in a Tijuana alley by a john who didn't like the blow job she'd given him. Roberto and me were just kids when it happened, but we got our revenge. My brother figured it all out, how to find the guy, then drug him so he couldn't fight back. Do you know what we did to him?"

Brognola shrugged.

"We cut his belly open and made him eat his own guts before we let him die." Murillo let this image sink in for a moment, then continued. "Our relatives were crazy, gas-sniffing, third-rate thieves and extortionists. Most of our uncles and cousins got butchered over women, money or drugs. They always seemed to be squashed flat by some bigger, meaner bastard. Roberto and me changed all that. We started doing the squashing and when we got rich enough, when we got enough power, we paid other guys to do it for us.

"Don Jorge wanted me to keep you alive," Murillo said. "He wants what you've got locked up in your head. But I don't care what Don Jorge wants."

Murillo looked at Brognola's upraised arm, the bruised fist clenched around the spike, the blood down the white wall. "Does that nail hurt?"

Before the big Fed could answer, he said, "Well, that's nothing compared to what I'm about to do to you."

A little closer, you sick bastard, Brognola thought. Come a little bit closer.

8

Bolan accelerated the Bronco toward the tight, right turn ahead. The yelling woman saw them coming up the hill. She was wearing a bright yellow cotton dress. She ran out from under the schoolhouse's metal awning, in the direction of the road.

No way could Bolan maintain the high rate of speed and keep all four wheels on the ground through the curve. Feathering the brakes, he forced the SUV into a curb-scraping arc. Even so, the four by four's tires squealed and it drifted sideways to the far side of the road.

As they roared past the schoolhouse, the woman waved her arms wildly over her head.

"She thinks we're some of Samosa's gunmen," the Texan said. "She knows where her bread gets buttered."

"Stop!" she bawled at them as she rounded the end of the planter.

Another second and she would have been in the middle of the street. The soldier looked in the rearview mirror to see her throw up her hands in despair.

"You should've shot her, too," the Texan told him, "the minute she opened her goddamned mouth. After the way you wasted all those cartel soldiers, pal, I can't believe you'd let a teacher get us both killed."

The Executioner's answer was to flatten the accelerator to the floorboard, making the big V-8 howl. The Bronco shot up the long, steep straightaway.

They were only about a quarter of the way up the hill, when a vehicle flew over the crest above them. It was one of the cartel Suburbans. Dark green with a smoke-tinted windshield. It was racing straight at them.

"Oh, shit," the cowboy groaned, violently rattling his handcuffs. "Oh, shit!"

Bolan didn't look to the left or right, didn't slow or swerve. There was nowhere to go but up. There really wasn't enough room on the street for both vehicles to pass safely. Not that he was thinking about safety.

When the Texan realized what was about to happen, what was certain to happen, he started to scream.

His voice sounded a lot like the teacher's.

At the last possible instant, when the two cars were no more than thirty feet apart, when Bolan could make out the faces of the two men in the front seat through the smoked-glass windshield, he cracked his door open and let himself roll out.

The pavement came up hard and fast.

Even though he protected his head with his arms as he bailed, the initial impact with the ground made him see stars. As he bounced out of control up the road, ten thousand pounds of SUV came together in a crash of ripping metal, shearing plastic and shattering glass.

Bolan came to a stop, facedown in the road, his back and arms pelted by bits of flying metal and glass. As he jumped to his feet, rising to a low crouch, he saw that the Suburban, being the heavier of the two vehicles, had won the chicken contest. Though the front ends of both cars were badly mangled, the Bronco was the one rolling slowly backward down the grade, and rapidly picking up speed as it did so.

The Executioner had to sprint to catch up to it. He jumped in around the door, then reached down and jerked up the emergency parking brake. The Bronco jerked to a stop.

On the passenger side, half hidden behind the deployed air bag, the cowboy dangled from the panic strap. His eyes were shut and his mouth hung open. Out cold.

Bolan grabbed the Colt M-16 and his pack from the back seat. As he ran uphill toward the stopped Suburban, he switched the assault rifle's selector from single to fullshot.

From fifty feet away, he could see that the head-on collision had made the Suburban's front air bags pop as well. The white bags practically filled the driver's compartment. Behind them, arms flailed frantically as the driver and his passenger struggled to get free.

Bolan freed them.

Pinning the M-16's trigger, he swept a line of 5.56 mm slugs across the smoky windshield. As the assault rifle stuttered, the glass spider-shattered and gave way, caving in on itself. The air bags popped. The heads popped. And the full-auto burst filled the front seat of the SUV with a bloody stew of shredded plastic, glass and bone fragments.

The drug soldiers in the middle and back seats of the Suburban weren't hampered by anything but their seat belts. The guy on the passenger side got his door open first.

Before the gunner could take a step, before he could clear his MAC-10 around the door, Bolan unleashed a short burst of tumblers, firing through the outside of the SUV's door. The slugs drove the drug soldier back into the door frame. His gun hand convulsed and the Ingram cut loose. Its muzzle was aimed straight down at his boots. Shot three times through the heart at close range, he was way too dead to care that he was blasting his own feet off.

The dead man's hand was still firing when the opposite

passenger's door and the Suburban's rear doors all swung open and three more armed soldiers jumped out.

Bolan dropped to one knee a second before the middle-seat passenger spun and opened fire, raking the inside of the SUV, trying to clip him with a wild, back-and-forth spray of slugs. Just over Bolan's head, flying bullets whined off the window frames and skipped off the tarmac into the hillside.

The Executioner dropped flat on the ground beside the Suburban's rocker panel. Because it was a four by four, it had great ground clearance. And in this case, that meant target acquisition. Turning onto his side, he shot the M-16 from the hip, nailing the shooter in both shins.

With a piercing shriek the guy twisted and fell, dropping his weapon to clutch at his shattered legs.

Bolan shot him once in the face, which stopped his screaming. Then he arced the rifle around to the rear, pinning the trigger, blowing out the back right tire an instant before he caught a second man's ankles with 5.56 mm slugs. Then the Colt's action locked back, mag spent.

Over the howling of the wounded drug thug from the other side of the Suburban, Bolan heard the sound of boots frantically slapping asphalt. The last guy was running uphill as fast as he could.

Standing, the Executioner dumped the empty magazine onto the ground and fished a fresh one from his pack. In a blur of smooth motion, he reloaded the weapon, chambered the first round and brought the assault rifle's butt up against his shoulder. Bracing against the roof of the SUV, he acquired the target in the Trijicon four-power and tapped out three tightly spaced single shots.

The running man sprawled on the road and, once down, he lay perfectly still.

No need for a follow-up.

The Executioner stepped around to the back of the SUV

and silenced the drug soldier's screams with a shot to the back of the neck. Then he turned and trotted back to the stalled Bronco. A torrent of fluid was leaking out from under its engine, oil and antifreeze pouring down the street.

"Get me the hell out of here!" the cowboy croaked as Bolan leaned in the Bronco's driver side. The whites of his eyes were pink, bloodshot from the force of the impact. Blood trickled from his nose and seeped from his wrists, soaking into the cuffs of his satin shirt. He started kicking his knees up against the underside of the air bag.

Bolan used his SOG Pentagon to slash open the air bag. As he reached to unlock the handcuffs from around the panic bar, the Texan suddenly went rigid, his reddened eyes bulging.

"Shit! Shit!" he moaned.

The Executioner looked up to see a second dark-green Suburban cresting the top of the hill and bearing down on them at high speed. A soldier in the SUV's front passenger's seat pulled himself halfway out the window, waving a submachine gun in his hand.

"For Pete's sake, hurry up!" the Texan cried.

Bolan got the key in the lock, but before he could turn it, the Bronco's windshield went opaque, and bullets screamed past his neck. Beneath the Executioner's outstretched hands, the cowboy's head slammed back into the headrest. Brains sprayed the headliner and back seat at the same instant the canvas-ripping sound of autofire reached them.

Bolan dived from the Bronco, pulling the M-16 off the driver's seat.

All around him slugs spanged into sheet metal and sparked off pavement. The guy hanging out of the Suburban's window was firing blind, scattering bullets, trying to panic his opponents.

Bolan was incapable of it.

He edged forward, kneeling beside the Bronco's front fender. Shouldering the Colt assault rifle, he took aim at the driver of the oncoming vehicle and in a single burst punched a tight cluster of crusty holes through the windshield.

Forty yards away, the Suburban swerved left, then hard right. Its horn sounded as it went out of control. A second later, it skidded off the road and crashed into the front of an adobe house.

Despite the front air bags, the driver of the Suburban flew right through the bullet-weakened windshield, landing on his chest on the hood, with his heels still inside the vehicle. His head had been turned into a faceless crater by the tightly grouped 5.56 rounds. On impact, the soldier shooting out the window went flying, too. His arms and legs flailed as, traveling fifty miles an hour, he went head-first into the house's front door.

No surprise, the door won.

As had happened before, the gunmen in the middle and rear seats jumped out of the crashed vehicle. But Bolan was too far away to use the same technique on them. From the distance of a hundred feet, the drug soldiers used the side of the SUV for cover and sprayed his position with concentrated full-auto fire.

The Executioner ducked behind the Bronco while it absorbed dozens of hits.

Getting pinned was part of his game plan. Bolan ripped a fragmentation grenade from his combat harness. He yanked the ring and let the grip safety flip off. Counting to three, he lobbed the grenade across the gap in a high arc.

The drug soldiers could see it coming.

The frag sailed over the roof of the Suburban and landed between it and the front of the adobe house. There was nowhere for the cartel crew to run, and no time. Because of the high arc, the grenade detonated with a solid *whack* and a burst of gray smoke an instant after it hit. The confined space magnified the concussion. Hot shrapnel clawed through the trapped soldiers, ripping them off their feet.

The two guys standing closest to the explosion didn't get up. They'd taken dozens of hits to their backs and heads. The other two gunmen staggered out from behind cover. Badly wounded and terrified, their clothes burning, they sprayed wild gunfire as they tried to retreat.

Bolan popped up and knocked them down with successive single shots.

Neat.

Quick.

Merciful.

He stripped the M-16's mag and replaced it with a full one. As he straightened, bullets started flying again. Slugs slapped the Bronco's front end, coring the already ruptured radiator, spanking into the windshield. Inside, the corpse of the Texan jerked and shuddered.

This time the firing was from the top of the road.

And the aim was better.

It was easy to see why. The third Suburban had stopped just short of the downhill grade. Its passengers had bailed out and taken up prone shooting positions on the crest of the hill, eighty yards away.

Bullets drummed the Bronco's hood, gouging long, ragged tears in it. Bolan smelled gasoline.

It was definitely time to move.

Under heavy fire, he sprinted across the road, ducked between two houses and into the jungle beyond.

The shooting stopped a few seconds later.

He beat his way through the dense bush, scrub trees and hanging vines, climbing a low rise. On the other side, the terrain dropped off precipitously, opening onto the ravine that bordered one side of the village and one side of the

Samosa hacienda. Confident of his direction and the location of his goal, Bolan forged ahead. Almost immediately he lost his footing on the wet leaves and vines and began slipping and sliding downhill. His fall was rapid and out of control.

When he slid past a game trail that ran perpendicular to the slope, he dug in the butt of the M-16 and managed to stop his descent. Rolling over, he crawled hand over hand back up to the trail. The track was hidden by the jungle canopy so it wasn't on the satellite recon map, but it seemed to be headed in the right direction, so he followed it. Almost at once, the path began to angle steeply up the slope. The ground was water-saturated, soft and treacherous, so he was careful.

After a few minutes of tough climbing, he could make out the rear of the houses that bordered the village square. A hundred and fifty feet above him, their back porches hung out over the ravine, standing on rickety looking, rough timber stilts and makeshift concrete pylons. He kept moving, trying to put as much overhead cover between himself and the porches as possible. Drug thugs firing from positions up there had a huge advantage, if they managed to spot him.

Coming around the base of a big tree, Bolan got his first look at the hacienda. It stood out on the end of a high promontory of jungle-covered rock. Its putty-colored exterior walls were fifteen feet high. Below the walls, the sides of the cliffs were nearly vertical. There was only one road.

A great place to make a stand.

The Executioner heard the *whup-whup-whup* of a helicopter. He didn't see it at first. Then, through the canopy of tree, he caught its windshield flash in the sun. It was spiraling away from the town at high speed. Somebody was leaving the party early.

He hoped to hell it wasn't Brognola.

Before he could take another step, a torrent of gunfire screamed down at him from above, from the back porches he could barely see.

9

Ramon Murillo kept his distance from Hal Brognola, staying just out of arm's reach, while he prattled on about revenge and impending torture. Brognola wasn't paying attention to anything the Mexican said. When he moved his right arm, he could feel his hand slip a little around the nail. Without the wide head to hold his palm in place, well-lubricated by blood, it was going to come off the spike like a lightning bolt.

The big Fed had already noted the side arm Murillo carried under his suit coat. The stainless steel Smith & Wesson automatic rode in a holster clipped over his trouser waistband. The only thing Brognola had going for him was surprise. No way would Murillo expect him to suddenly have the use of both his arms and to be free from the wall. But to maximize that slender advantage, he knew he had to be near enough to get his hands on the bastard.

Murillo's black eyes glittered as he said, "You'll fight me to keep the other two nails from going in, but in the end, like all the rest, you will lose. Like the others, you'll struggle as hard as you can for as long as you can. After a while you'll become exhausted, weak as a kitten. Sometimes it takes as long as fifteen minutes for me to gain complete control. With you, I think five or six minutes is closer to the mark. You don't look in that good a shape. After I get you hung up by the other nails, the retribution for my brother's death will begin...."

Murillo reached for the side pocket of his suit jacket, fumbling around the long wooden handle of the framing hammer that stuck out of it. From the pocket he took out a thick metal spike and showed it to Brognola.

To Brognola it looked like a landscape nail, hacked off at a length of about six inches, and the point rehoned on a grinding wheel.

Murillo put the ball of his thumb to the tip and tested it. "Seems nice and sharp to me." He leaned forward, offering it to his captive. "Maybe you want to try?"

Instead, Brognola tried to kick him in the kidney, an effort that nearly cost him his balance on the orange crate. Murillo sensed the strike coming and easily moved out of the way.

"You need a longer leg, Fed," the Mexican said, laughing. "About four feet longer."

"Bastard!" Brognola snarled at him, impotently.

But he was playacting. Under the facade of fear and panic, Brognola was the one in charge of the game. He wanted to make his torturer think he'd seen the limits of his maneuverability and coordination. He wanted him to be confident, reckless.

Murillo placed the spike between his teeth and made a sudden grab for the Fed's left arm.

Brognola pulled it back, out of the way, and Three Nails came after it, lunging with both hands.

Brognola let him catch his wrist.

At that critical moment, the sound of gunfire rattled the room's windows. The loud crackling came from the road leading up to the village.

Gripping Brognola's wrist between his hands, Murillo glanced over at the windows. It was a natural reflex.

Brognola didn't have time to consider the reason for the shooting. All that mattered was that the sudden noise distracted Murillo for a split second. A split second was all he needed.

Brognola jerked his palm off the nail and lunged from the crate, driving with his legs. As he did so, he locked his arms around the startled Mexican's shoulders and used all of his weight and momentum to wrestle the guy to the floor. Brognola landed on top with a bone-jarring thud. Beneath him, he could feel the breath whoosh out of Murillo.

The tables had turned.

Slamming his right forearm into the back of Murillo's neck, he bore down hard to pin his head to the floor, while he dug in his pants pocket for the minihacksaw. Forcing the man's mouth against the hardwood, he reached under his chin with the six-inch serrated blade.

A blade not meant for stabbing.

Because of the stress of the situation and the mortal danger, because of the pain he'd suffered, because his experience as a hand-to-hand fighter was limited, Brognola wasn't thinking clearly.

He slashed the minihack across the drug smuggler's throat, using it like a knife.

Murillo let out a shrill cry and began to struggle wildly.

A hacksaw wasn't made to cut throats. With its fine teeth, Brognola's weapon of desperation had made nothing more than a shallow notch in Murillo's flesh. It was meant to cut cheap steel with a lot of rapid back-and-forth movement.

When Brognola started doing that, trying his damnedest to saw through the front of Murillo's throat, his former torturer went berserk, bucking, kicking, trying to twist away.

Brognola seized hold of the back of his head by the greasy mop of coarse black hair and smashed his forehead into the floor. He did this over and over as hard as he could.

When Murillo stopped fighting him, Brognola tossed away the minihacksaw and pulled the framing hammer from Murillo's pocket. The big Fed wasn't really thinking; he was reacting. He wanted the man dead, needed the man dead. Rearing up, he swung the heavy hammer down with everything he had. It made a hollow *thunk* as its face punched through the top of the Mexican's skull. Brognola jerked the hammerhead free and, as he did, bright arterial blood spurted high in the air. Brognola hit him twice more, burying the hammer in the center of his head, mushing his brains. Blood from the horrendous wound gushed over the floor. Murillo's heart was still pumping. His legs began to jerk.

Brognola trapped the man under the weight of his body, holding him still while the life ran out.

It took about a minute for his heart to pump itself dry. And when it was over, when Brognola was sure it was over, only then did he let go.

Pushing to his feet, Brognola rolled Murillo onto his back, into the spreading pool of blood. For a moment, he stared at the gaping mouth, the protruding tongue, the dead eyes.

His veins still choked with adrenaline, his hands shaking on the gory hammer, Brognola heard himself snarl, "How about that, asshole?"

Brognola dropped the hammer, then he bent and reached inside the suit jacket with his good hand and pulled out the man's handgun. As Brognola straightened, the awful coppery smell overwhelmed him and the room began to spin. Lurching away from the corpse, he stumbled to the nearest corner and leaning a shoulder against the wall, dry-heaved.

"Oh, God," he moaned. "God!"

When the spasms passed, he staggered to the door. He tried to shift the pistol to his right hand and found that he couldn't control the weapon that way. His injured hand had lost most of its strength. The left would have to do, even though he wasn't much of an ambidextrous shooter. If it came down to a gunfight between him and the soldiers guarding the hacienda, Brognola knew he was bound to lose, anyway.

As he stepped cautiously into the hallway, the continuing clatter of gunfire from the road was interrupted by the unmistakable sound of a detonating hand grenade.

There was a war going on outside.

The thought brought a smile to his lips.

The Executioner had arrived and he was painting the town red.

Hal followed the short hallway to its end, where it joined a stairwell leading down. Apparently, he was in the hacienda's attic. Holding the Smith & Wesson braced in both hands, he quickly descended to the first landing. Though he was ready to shoot, if at all possible, he wanted to get out of the building without firing the weapon. If he had to use the gun to defend himself, it would bring the already-alerted drug soldiers down on him in a big hurry.

Pausing at the corner of the landing, he could hear shouting from the house below and the heavy tramp of running feet. He listened hard. No one seemed to be heading his way. For the moment at least, he had been forgotten, or maybe Ramon Murillo had given orders that they weren't to be disturbed, no matter what happened. The gunmen downstairs would have expected the sounds of Murillo's fun and games—the struggle, the screams, the thud of blows—from the attic room, if not the final outcome.

His weapon pointed ahead and down, Brognola descended the next flight of steps. There was no landing at the bottom this time. The staircase ended in another hallway. He poked his head out of the stairwell, then pulled back. A main hallway, from the look of it. Its opposite side was open. There was no interior wall, only a waist-high carved hardwood balcony rail. He looked out again, checking the carpeted hallway in both directions. It was deserted. A dozen rooms opened into it, all the doors shut.

On the other side of the banister was open air. A couple hundred feet away, across the void, he could see the opposite end of the building, and another open-sided hallway, just like this one. No one was moving over there, either.

Because he'd been blindfolded when he'd been brought into the place, he hadn't seen the inside of the hacienda before. It was two stories down to the ground level and a huge, central, marble-floored room, decorated with a collection of antique furniture, sculptures and paintings. It all looked very old and very rich.

Brognola drew back from the railing as a group of drug soldiers appeared directly below him. They sprinted into the big room, heading for an arched doorway at one end. They didn't look up.

Brognola leaned against the beam, pondering his next move. He didn't know the floor plan of the hacienda and he didn't know where the guards were stationed. Those two facts put him at a serious disadvantage.

"What are you doing loose?" said a gruff voice behind him.

The choice was taken out of his hands.

Brognola whirled around just in time to see 250 pounds of cartel thug charging for him. The guy hadn't seen his weapon, and didn't expect to find him armed. It didn't matter that Brognola wasn't used to shooting with his left hand, the range to target was only a foot and a half. The weapon in his fist cracked three times.

They were practically nose to nose when the Mexican's

face contorted in a grimace of pain, eyes squeezed shut, teeth bared, tendons in his neck standing out. He let out a gust of garlic breath as his knees buckled. Hands clutching his chest, he brushed by Brognola, hit the railing and dropped to the carpet.

The pistol's reports were deafening, booming through the big house.

Shouts erupted from the room below. When Brognola looked over the rail, he saw drug soldiers pointing up at him. A bunch of them split up and started running for opposite staircases to flank and trap him in the third-story hallway.

One glance told Brognola that more men were coming up the stairs after him than were staying down to guard the ground floor. There were just two guys left downstairs. They stood in front of a huge flagstone fireplace. They were pointing their handguns at him, but they didn't fire.

Nobody had touched off a shot at him, yet.

Were they under orders from Don Jorge Samosa to keep him alive at all costs?

Maybe they didn't want to put holes in the expensive antiques.

Brognola waited a full minute, listening to the running feet on the steps, letting his pursuers reach the second floor, then he put a leg over the railing and jumped.

10

Las Cruces shipyard, main dock, 9:04 a.m.

Trevor Eames watched from the viewing stand, his head throbbing to the beat of a military band, as Admiral Fuentes helped a petite, pretty young woman dressed in a lime-green Jackie-O pillbox hat, matching suit and heels crack a ribbon-suspended bottle of Moët champagne across the towering bow of the seventy-meter *Bernardo Chinle*. The woman was the admiral's third wife, and twenty-five years his junior. A second or two later, the semidisplacement steel hull slid down the launch ramp and into the water.

The admiral turned to the other dignitaries, threw open his arms and said, "It floats!"

Fuentes got a big laugh from the handful of bureaucrats, elected officials and corporate representatives who were present. Eames could barely manage a smile. He had been praying, in fact, that the drug-interdiction vessel would sink the instant it hit the water. Such a thing wasn't unheard-of. Ships had been known to go down almost immediately after launching. If the *Bernardo Chinle* had sunk in the Las Cruces marina basin, an act of God instead of sabotage, he would have been off the hook.

It took a few minutes for the shipyard employees to work the mooring lines, and a few more to get the gangway connected to the accommodation ladder on the vessel's starboard flank.

The DIV's twenty-four-man skeleton crew stood at attention on the dock, single file, shoulder to shoulder, their duffle bags at their feet. Carrying only his attaché case, Eames walked past the row of beaming, dungaree-uniformed, mostly teenaged sailors, grateful that the sea trials called for less than the vessel's normal complement of sixty to eighty men. Seeing the crew lined up like that, sensing their excitement, Eames began to feel the true weight of what he was about to do. He didn't look any of the sailors in the eye.

He couldn't.

They were all as good as dead.

Eames boarded the ship ahead of the seamen and immediately started walking toward the bow. Its above-water superstructure was aluminum, constructed of obliquely angled plates like a Stealth fighter jet, and painted with the same dark-gray energy-absorbing material. This design made the DIV virtually invisible to radar, which allowed it to sneak up on drug-running surface vessels and submarines.

The cutter-style hull had two above-main-deck levels. One up from the main deck contained the crew's quarters. Aft on that same level was the hangar and landing platform designed for a French Puma attack helicopter. The landing deck was vacant as the aircraft hadn't shown up from the manufacturer, yet. The second level held the bridge, with its high-tech integrated propulsion and weapons systems.

Most of the crew that boarded behind him turned off, climbing the stairs to the first level, heading for their quarters to stow gear. Eames walked farther forward and mounted the two flights of steps to the bridge deck, which he entered through a side door.

The *Bernardo Chinle's* bridge looked like something out

of *Star Trek*. Its chest-high, operations center was constructed in a half-octagon shape. On the left side was the navigation suite, which was lined with phase array, Sperry vision system units, over-the-horizon radars, ADG-3000 autopilots, ring laser gyrops, and multiple mil-spec GPS receivers. The computers had adaptive artificial intelligence. Their fuzzy-logic processors were capable of extremely accurate course predictions, based on constantly updated evaluations of sea state, drift, current and true speed over ground.

Dead center in the half octagon was the propulsion control desk, with banks of computer screens and a pair of helm joysticks, which replaced a ship's wheel for steering. On the right side were the weapons systems, communications and sonar. By touching the keypads built onto the screens, the fire control officer designated targets for the ship's batteries of guided missiles.

Thanks to the DIV's fully automated, integrated bridge, a crew of six to eight could control the 230-foot vessel in normal patrol and interdiction operations. Because of the high degree of automation, whether that crew cooperated or not, it would only take three men to steal it.

As Eames took his chair behind the propulsion desk, Admiral Oswaldo Fuentes entered the bridge. He was like a kid with a new toy. He was actually rubbing his hands together in excitement.

"You're looking a little unsteady this morning," he said to Eames in a good-natured way, not really concerned. "Too much of that damned El Gato Negro. I warned you about that."

"I'm fine, Admiral. Really. Just a bit of a hangover, but I took some aspirin."

"Good. Then why don't you start them up?"

Eames tapped a code onto the screen's keypad. Seconds later, the deck underfoot shuddered as the big mills cranked over. Once running, the vibration leveled out and became a faint, steady hum.

As Eames monitored the computer-simulated gauges and dials, the Mexican helmsman took the seat next to him, behind the array of joysticks.

The indicators on the computer screen showed normal function. When initiated, the start-up sequence for the twin 6000-horsepower engines was fully automated; barring some difficulty, it took about five minutes from beginning to end. Everything went smoothly. All sensors and pumps were fully operational, and air pressure in the control lines was steady within established parameters.

When the start-up routine had concluded, Eames said, "You have full power available, Admiral."

Fuentes stepped to the bridge's front window, hands clasped behind his back. Looking out over the bow, he rocked a little on his heels, savoring the sensation. This was his crowning glory. The other ships in the Mexican navy were cast-offs, secondhand, obsolete garbage donated mostly by the U.S. The *Bernardo Chinle* was the first truly modern state-of-the-art attack ship ever produced by his country. And he was the proud papa.

"Let's take her out for a spin," he said. "Give the signal to cast off the mooring lines."

When this was done, the admiral said, "Back us out of here, Helmsman."

The sailor turned in his chair and said, "Señor Eames, will you please give me one-quarter power on the aft starboard thruster, one-eighth on the starboard bow."

The moment of truth was fast approaching. Eames keyed in the control sequences for the side thrusters that allowed the big ship to maneuver into and out of tight places. The space to turn in the marina was limited by landward breakwaters and by a sandbar off the stern.

As the ship rapidly arced away from the dock out into

the bay, the sailor manning the sonar array announced, "Admiral, the shoal water is coming up quickly."

The helmsman said, "Cut the thrusters and give me port engine, one quarter forward."

Truth time had arrived.

Already committed to another course of action, Eames gave him full reverse, both engines.

The huge vessel surged backward.

Admiral Fuentes staggered away from the windows, grabbing a handrail to keep from falling.

When they hit the sandbar an instant later, the shock broke the admiral's grip and drove him to his knees on the bridge's deck. The crunch of impact was followed by the awful grinding vibration of the props beating against something solid.

At once, Fuentes sprang to his feet, absolutely livid. His face turned purple, and his big hands clenched into fists. For the first time, Eames heard the man curse.

He had good reason.

Not a thousand yards from the launch dock, within the first few minutes of operation, in full view of the very important guests still milling around the reviewing stand, the crew had managed to ground the vessel.

Eames immediately disengaged the propellers to keep them from being damaged.

The helmsman let go of the joystick like it was the head of a rattlesnake. He pushed back into his chair, throwing up his hands as if to say, Hey, it wasn't my fault.

"Can we get free?" Fuentes snarled at them.

"I'm working on it, sir," Eames said.

"Is there any damage?"

"I'm checking, Admiral."

"It's only sand, goddammit! Get us off this fucking bar!"

"I'm on top of it," Eames said. "Just give me a minute or two."

IGNACIO NUÑEZ sat in a folding lawnchair on top of the wheelhouse of the shrimper *Bahia Magdalena*. In a battered straw cowboy hat and swimming trunks, he watched the launch of the DIV through a pair of very expensive, high-powered binoculars. He was flanked on both sides by platoons of pelicans. They perched shoulder to shoulder on the boat's outrigger lines. The building heat of the day was making the shrimp boat under him smell worse and worse, a combination of rotten shellfish and bird shit.

A breeze would have been nice.

But Nuñez could handle the smell. For what he and his team were being paid for the day's work, he would have gladly puckered up and kissed the ass of every pelican on board.

When the dockside DIV's engines started up and black smoke began pouring from its stack, Nuñez rose from his chair and stepped to the far side of the wheelhouse. On the main deck below, hidden from view, seven men in scuba gear relaxed along the starboard rail. In addition to the usual mask, fins and compressed air tanks, each man wore a waterproof chest pack, containing a suppressor-equipped 9 mm Heckler & Koch MP-5 and three extra 30-round stick magazines.

He gave them the thumbs-up signal, then turned and climbed down the ladder to the main deck.

As he strapped on his own scuba tank, the others went over the rail, one by one. They swam close to the side of the boat, treading water, waiting for their leader to join them.

Nuñez and his Panamanian team had received their SEAL training in San Diego two years earlier, at U.S. taxpayers' expense. For their considerable investment of sweat and pain, the Panamanians had expected long and distinguished careers in their own navy. But when Panama had disbanded its military, it no longer needed a special forces unit. Tossed out on the street, literally, they had sold themselves to the highest bidder. They had become mercenaries for Don Jorge Luis Samosa.

After pulling on his weapon pack, Nuñez entered the water in a backward roll. Clearing his mask of water, he dived, swimming under the barnacle-encrusted keel of the shrimper. Reaching the other side, he swam just beneath the surface, moving steadily toward the middle of the bay.

Because it was Mexico, the sandbar that was their destination had no floating hazard marker. But the water was so clear that Nuñez could see the white shelf rising out of the depths beneath him. When the distance to the bottom was no more than twenty feet, he led the other swimmers down to it.

As they regrouped in the middle of the sandbar, the DIV was already backing away from the pier. They saw the *Bernardo Chinle* coming, a dim, impossibly huge, gray mass. When the ship full-reversed onto the edge of the sandbar, they felt the rocking jolt through the sand, then the pounding roar of the grounded props.

The instant the prop noise died, Nuñez started swimming upward as fast as he could, toward the great shadow looming ahead. His men followed in tight formation behind him. Timing was critical, a matter of life and death. His underwater team had to get to their destination before the gigantic propellers restarted. If they didn't, they would be sucked in by the wash and turned into bloody pulp.

Nuñez surfaced at the end of the ramp. He spit out his regulator and pushed his mask down around his neck. The steel ramp, though dry, was slick as well as steep, and it took some serious effort to haul himself onto the ship. He used the deep groove in the middle of the chute, which protected the outdrive from damage during launch and retrieval, to get a grip and foothold.

He crawled hand over hand up the ramp. Taking a length of line from his weight belt, he fastened it to one of the cleats, then tossed the free end down the ramp to his waiting men.

As they pulled themselves up in turn, Nuñez looked over the craft as he stripped off the scuba gear.

All of the Panamanian SEAL team had reached the loading platform when the DIV's engines roared and the vessel jerked violently to the right. The water off the end of the ramp churned into head-high foam. After a pause, the ship jerked again as a second blast of power was applied to the grounded props. Then, with a short, low-pitched groan, the stern came unstuck from the sandbar.

As the *Bernardo Chinle* steamed ahead, toward the bay entrance and the Pacific, Nuñez watched the last of his men dump their gear and take their submachine guns out of the chest packs. Everything had been rehearsed dozens of times.

With a curt hand signal, he ordered two SEALs to stand guard on both sides of the bulkhead door at the end of the launch platform. Hand signals were necessary because, with the engines going full bore and the mouth of the bay open to the props, it was impossible to hear. He checked his diver's watch for the elapsed time. They had to wait fifteen more minutes before they could advance, to give the DIV time to get out to sea.

Ten minutes into the wait, without warning, the bulkhead door swung inward. Two Mexican sailors, only half paying attention to where they were going, and never suspecting what they were about to stumble onto, stepped over the raised sill of the watertight door. When the first man through the door saw the five armed strangers and the pile of discarded scuba gear on the deck, he came to such a sudden stop that the second sailor ran right into his back.

The Panamanians standing on either side of the door rushed forward and jammed the muzzles of their SMGs into the back of the sailors' heads. In shock and disbelief, the two Mexicans raised their hands. Then the taller one sank slowly to his knees, his eyes full of fear. The other one just stared slack-jawed at all the guns pointed at him. He looked to be the oldest of the pair, maybe nineteen years old.

The captured sailors asked for no explanation, though they had to be mystified as to who their attackers were and what their goals might be. It was a question of power. The Mexicans knew they had none. They realized without having to be told that their lives hung on a whim, and that knowledge rendered them speechless and compliant.

Ordinarily, Nuñez would have ordered the sailors killed on the spot, or better yet, done the job himself, but this mission had some very special requirements. Special requirements were what made it pay so well.

Executing the Mexicans would've meant finding a secure place to stow their bodies. He couldn't just slide the corpses down the launch chute into the water, and he couldn't leave them lying on the platform where, when the ship was scuttled, they could get loose and float to the surface. Nuñez's orders were that no signs of the ship were to be left. Debris was to be reduced to an absolute minimum. No drifting bodies. To guarantee that, the first part of the operation called for the live capture and containment of the entire skeleton crew. Every man was to be accounted for. The Panamanian SEALs had orders to open fire on the Mexicans only if the mission's success or their lives were directly threatened.

Nuñez pointed his finger at the standing sailor, then pointed down at the deck. The man dropped to his knees beside his friend. They both put their hands behind their necks and laced their fingers. The Mexican navy had taught them how to surrender, if nothing else.

The younger of the two began to pray. Nuñez could read his lips as they moved. The sailor was asking the Virgin Mary for deliverance in this, the hour of his death.

For five more minutes, they waited in silence. Then Nuñez led them through the watertight door and down a corridor. The Mexican sailors were forced to walk in the middle of the pack, at gunpoint and completely surrounded. With the bulkhead door closed behind them, the noise of the engine decreased markedly. It was so quiet Nuñez could hear one of the Mexicans sniffling and sobbing behind him.

No one said a word.

They all knew exactly what they had to do.

The corridor connected to a wider hallway that ran past the engine room. Nuñez hadn't planned on stopping and taking more prisoners. His goal was to reach the bridge as quickly as possible without raising an alarm. Prisoners would only slow them. But the engine room door opened when he was about five feet from it, and he was left with no choice.

An older Mexican sailor, with a paunch and a weather-seamed face, stepped out into the corridor. Nuñez moved cat-quick, closing the distance and smashing the side of his MP-5 across the man's forehead. It made a hollow sound against his skull.

The sailor staggered back against the wall, clutching his face. Blood squirted out from between his fingers.

Nuñez kept on moving. The Panamanians marching behind him jerked the injured sailor into line beside the other captives and when he dawdled, moaning over his wound, they booted him along ahead of them.

The team reached the stairway amidships without seeing

another Mexican. A minute later, Nuñez had cleared the top of the stairs and was shoving open the watertight door. Stepping onto the main deck, turning for the bow, he broke into a jog.

Straight ahead, he could see the length of the ship's rail, all the way to the end of the bridge tower. About twenty yards away, at the foot of the stairway to the bridge, three sailors were looking over the side, smiling, laughing. In what seemed like slow motion, they turned their heads toward the stern.

What they saw made them freeze. It took them only a second to realize that the ship was under attack. Then they tried to dart across the deck for the staircase.

It was only fifteen feet.

It might as well have been a mile.

Nuñez brought his H&K up to hip height and touched off a short full-auto burst. In the open air, with the wind rushing over the deck, the sound of the engines and the sea, the sound-suppressed gunfire was inaudible. With the superstructure on the right and railing on the left, it was like shooting down a bowling alley lane. The sailors went sprawling to the deck. The near misses scored bright gouges in the superstructure's gray antiradar finish.

The killing meant a little more work for Nuñez's men, who would now have to lug the bodies below decks, but for the mission to succeed, the bridge had to be taken by surprise. It was imperative that no distress call be sent out. The mission was supposed to look routine. No one was to come looking for the ship before the SEALs sent it to the bottom. And no one was to know what happened to it afterward.

Nuñez hopped over the still-jerking bodies of the fallen sailors and vaulted up the steps to the bridge.

As THE *Bernardo Chinle* motored due west, Trevor Eames kept glancing at his Rolex, wondering if the Panamanians had gotten safely on board. Their window of opportunity was narrow. If they had swum too slowly, or if something had delayed their departure from the shrimper, they could have gotten caught in the props when he restarted them.

If the Panamanians didn't hold up their end, would he be blamed for the result?

Eames knew the answer.

Samosa's men would kill him, on the off chance he had shaved some time off the grounding on purpose. The only way he was going to escape with a whole skin was if the mission went exactly as planned.

In the meantime, Admiral Fuentes was still bristling over the accidental grounding. His customary good humor had deserted him. Perhaps he thought the incident might be a bad omen.

If that was the case, he was right.

The port door to the bridge burst open and four men armed with submachine guns rushed in. The paramilitaries were followed by three Mexican crewmen, obviously prisoners. Entering behind the sailors were four more gunmen, who quickly spread out along the bridge's front wall to completely cover the room.

Admiral Fuentes was astonished by the intruders' sudden entrance, as were the rest of the bridge crew.

"Everybody stay right where you are, and put your hands in the air," the leader of the gunmen said. He was a dark-skinned Hispanic man with thinning, curly black hair worn short. He was dressed only in wet swimming trunks. "I will kill anyone who doesn't show me both palms, right now."

The bridge crew was unarmed. Because it was just a shakedown cruise, all of the ship's weapons were still secured in the armory, under lock and key on the first level.

"What is this about?" Fuentes demanded of the man who had given the order.

Ignacio Nuñez raised the muzzle of his H&K and without a word of explanation or warning opened fire at extreme close range into the chest of the Mexican officer who was standing across from him.

Captain Ricardo Elizondo jerked backward like a puppet, his arms thrown high in the air, bits of meat flying out his back, the 9 mm rounds cracking the DIV's front window. Elizondo crashed to the deck in a lifeless heap.

"That's what it's about," Nuñez said to Fuentes. "Now get on the horn and order all the crew to assemble on the forecastle. Do it now!"

"You won't get away with this," the admiral said.

"Do it or I shoot two more."

Eames could see the fury in Fuentes' eyes as he grabbed the ship's intercom microphone. It made his mouth go dry.

The admiral spoke into the mike, telling the crew to go immediately to the forward deck and await orders.

The Panamanian didn't look at Eames as he stepped over to the navigation console. He passed the sailor sitting in front of the GPS a slip of paper with a set of map coordinates written on it.

"Plot a course for that position," Nuñez said. He watched over the man's shoulder as he tapped in the numbers. "Bring the ship around to our new course," he ordered the helmsman. To Eames he said, "I want maximum speed from the engines."

"Where are you taking my ship?" Fuentes demanded.

"It's not your ship anymore. It's been confiscated."

Nuñez moved down the line to the sailor manning the fire control and electronic countermeasures panel.

"I want you to shut down all communications, ship to ship, ship to shore," he said. "I want this done immediately. I want the radar jamming system activated in four minutes. Full countermeasures. We'll be running in ghost mode.''

"Where are you taking us?" Fuentes said. Despite the orders not to move, the admiral stepped around the half-octagon control suite and looked at the GPS-satellite map of their projected course and destination. "That's no-where!" he exclaimed.

"It's 1500 fathoms of nowhere, to be precise," Nuñez said. With the barrel of his SMG, he pointed at the built-in couch behind the nav station. "Go sit over there," he told the admiral. "If you get up before I tell you to, I'll put holes through *your* nice white shirt, too."

One of the Panamanian SEALs who was watching the sailors line up on the forecastle, turned away from the bridge's front window and said, "There are eighteen men down there. That's the lot."

Nuñez made a hand gesture, and four of the gunmen left the bridge. Seconds later, down on the foredeck, they had the sailors corralled and were forcing them to march, hands on top of their heads, single file back along the first level.

Eames knew they were about to be locked in the hold of the ship, sealed behind watertight doors. They would never see daylight again.

"What's our ETA?" Nuñez asked the navigator.

The sailor read off the computer's running estimate. "We'll be at the coordinates in forty-five minutes."

"That's just perfect," Nuñez said. "I want everyone to relax and enjoy the ride."

11

Hacienda Corto de Vista

Don Jorge shepherded his boys ahead of him, under the beating rotors of the Sikorsky helicopter and through its open rear door. Because of the blade noise directly overhead, the drug lord couldn't hear the head-on car crash on the road leading up to the village. He didn't notice the crackle of automatic weapons fire that followed the crash, either.

After belting the boys into their seats, he reached forward and tapped the pilot on the shoulder. It was the signal to go. As Samosa fastened his own safety harness, the Sikorsky lifted off from the hacienda's landing pad, hurtling away from the hilltop village and turning in a broad sweeping arc back toward Mazatlán.

Had they overflown the hamlet, they would have certainly seen the wrecked cars and the strewed bodies.

As it was, his main concern as they headed west was how unusually withdrawn his sons seemed. They were no doubt still suffering from the loss of their mother. They were still quite young and impressionable, and deep wounds didn't heal quickly, if ever.

That he might have injured Juanito and Pedro by his actions disturbed him greatly, yet Samosa had no doubt that he had followed the only course open to him. And in the long run, he believed he had done the best thing for his boys. It was important to him that they follow in his footsteps. Otherwise, the empire he had spent his life building would, upon his death, collapse into chaos.

He had tried to begin preparing his boys for the task by cultivating in them what he recognized as his own strong points. They were what had always separated him from the rest of the criminal pack. The Lord of the Seas was a murderer, a thief, a slave-maker, but he was also a genius. He was smart enough to never have left a trail for law enforcement to follow. Smart enough to have corrupted the police forces of five nations. Smart enough to hold together the disparate and factionalized elements of his cartel: growers, processors and distributors. He had a knack for seeing opportunities before others did, and he had the courage to seize his chance when it appeared. He had never backed down from another man. Not once. Not even from his own father.

It was more than simple stubbornness.

More than arrogance.

He had to be in control of everything within his reach.

That Yovana Ortiz, his one-time mistress, had taken their children from him was something he couldn't abide. It went against his nature. Even if she had never given evidence against his cartel, he would have had her killed for stealing the boys.

Samosa pushed back in his seat and stretched his legs. It was good that his sons would see the sinking of the big Mexican ship. Not merely as an entertainment, though it would certainly be that. Juanito and Pedro had no conception of how much money he was going to send to the bottom of the sea, this day. Even if he told them, it would make no real impression. But the size of the ship, its newness, its perfection would impress them. It was important that they understood the extent of the cartel's power, of his power. And that they should never be afraid of exercising it themselves.

The drug lord glanced over at his oldest son, who was staring out the window. Juanito's face looked boyish and round, but the eyes...the eyes.

It was like looking into a mirror and seeing his own reflection.

It made him feel both humble and intensely proud.

I have so many things to teach you, Samosa thought.

12

Hacienda Corto de Vista

Hal Brognola started second-guessing himself the moment he pushed off from the railing. It turned out that it was one thing to visualize the two-floor drop, and another thing altogether to see the ground rushing up at him, the air buffeting his face. The wrought-iron-framed antique French daybed looked mighty tiny when Brognola launched himself at it.

People died from two-story falls all the time.

His feet hit the sofa dead center. The double mattress and springs swallowed up his feet, ankles and calves without really slowing him. Then the hundred-year-old bed frame let out a shriek, its spot welds and flat springs popping loose, and it collapsed in on itself. The sofa's underside hit the floor an instant before Brognola did.

As he rolled off the pile of wreckage, he let out a groan. Caught up in the tangle of stuffing, springs and bent wrought iron, his right ankle twisted before it came free. The pain shot up his leg all the way to the hip. Even so, he managed to fight through it and swing the Smith & Wesson pistol's sights onto the closest targets.

The two guys standing by the fireplace were just as surprised as Brognola was by what he'd done. And that he was now aiming a gun at them.

Before they could scatter, Brognola braced his weak

hand's wrist against the bed frame and started squeezing the trigger. His first two shots sailed high, sparking off the flagstone mantle above the drug soldiers' heads. The third bullet flew between them, entered the firebox, hit something inside, caromed around and ricocheted back out again. Its reverse track carried it through the chest of the soldier on the right. Knocked a stumbling step forward, the cartel thug looked down at his T-shirt in amazement. A ragged hole below his breastbone gushed a torrent of bright blood.

Clutching at the wound to try to stop the flow, the gunman thought about raising his weapon and returning fire. Or maybe it was just a reflex action. He got the pistol halfway up, then his eyelids closed and he toppled sideways to the floor.

The other drug soldier ducked out of sight behind an ornately carved sideboard. Brognola fired as he tracked the presumed path of the gunman from right to left, blowing holes in the drawers and cabinet doors from one end of the piece of furniture to the other.

After the fourth shot, he heard a groan from the other side.

Either he'd hit him or the guy was faking it, trying to get him to come closer. Before he could make sure, gunfire rattled down at him from the third-floor balcony. The volley of triangulated fire crashed the pottery urns beside the daybed, turning them into ceramic shrapnel. The raging bullets chewed holes in the Persian carpets and decapitated a marble bust of a Greek goddess.

Having seen Brognola wax a couple of their own right under their noses, the cartel drug soldiers weren't too concerned about keeping their boss's possessions intact.

Brognola held the Smith over his head and sprayed a few unaimed shots in the direction of the balcony to give himself some cover. Then he heaved himself up and hopping on his one good foot, half dragging the other, he moved under the overhang of the second-floor balcony. By doing this, he managed to get momentarily out of the line of fire.

As he scurried to cover, he tried to remember how many gunmen he'd seen coming after him before he jumped. Was it six or seven? He had no idea how many of the opposition were in the hacienda, but did it really matter?

There was no way he could plan an exit strategy under the circumstances. He didn't know the floor plan of the hacienda. He just had to pick a direction at random and fight his way along it, to react to whatever situation confronted him, assuming sooner or later he'd either run out of ammunition or find an escape route.

From above he heard the sound of running feet on the stairs. There was no time to rest his ankle. Brognola gritted his teeth and hobbled as fast as he could through the nearest doorway. It opened into a short corridor, which in turn opened onto the hacienda's kitchen.

Brognola pushed into the white, high-ceilinged room. The countertops were also white tile. There was a row of tall windows along the far wall, which allowed tropical sunlight to flood the work area.

At first, Brognola thought the place was deserted, but as he hopped forward, a Mexican man in a cook's uniform with a food-stained apron jumped out from behind a butcher-block-topped cutting table. He had a big cleaver in one hand and a skinned rabbit by the feet in the other.

He wasn't alone.

Behind him were two women, also dressed in white, with black hair nets. They clung to the cook's arms, their brown fingers dusted with flour.

For a second the big Fed thought he was going to have to shoot the wild-eyed bastard. And he was ready to do it, if necessary. But the cook didn't want to fight. Brognola could see it in his face. The poor guy just wanted to get the hell out with his girlfriends or sisters or cousins. Throwing the knife and the rabbit onto the floor, the cook backed up, waving his empty hands in the air. Then the three of them turned and ran.

Brognola assumed that they were heading for the nearest exit and he hopped after them, wincing every time he put weight on his bad ankle.

He couldn't move fast enough.

He only got as far as the brushed stainless steel door of the walk-in freezer when he heard the tramp of feet in the corridor between the main room and the kitchen. He opened the freezer door a crack. A light came on inside.

Leaving the door ajar, he moved to the doorway the cook and his helpers had darted through. Beyond it was a storeroom with shelves stacked with cans and bottles. At the far end was a door. Brognola knew he couldn't cover the length of the room before the drug soldiers overran him. Not on the bad foot. He would get shot in the back, for sure. He leaned out of sight against the wall beside the doorway.

Holding his breath, the big Fed listened as hard as he could. He heard whispers and the creak of shoe leather coming from the kitchen. He counted at least two, maybe three of the enemy approaching.

The question was, were they focused on the freezer, or not?

Brognola took a firm, two-handed grip on the Smith, exhaled, then poked his head around the door frame.

There were four of them, not three.

One had taken hold of the freezer's handle. Another soldier had his back pressed against the front of the re-frigeration unit, his pistol pointed in the air, ready to cover the inside of the freezer when the door opened wide enough. The other two thugs stood ten feet away, their automatic weapons angled to give the first man into the freezer covering fire, if necessary.

The guy on the door jerked it back.

The man by the freezer wall spun around, pointing his gun through the open door, then scooted inside, out of view. The two men on backup shifted their positions slightly to get clear firing lanes into the thirty-foot cold room.

Brognola brought the Smith up and shot the nearest hardman through the throat. The gunshot boomed in the tile room. Even as the man jolted sideways, dropping his submachine gun, the big Fed rode the recoil wave onto his next target. His face and neck spattered with the falling guy's blood, the second hardman whirled around in a panic. His finger was stuck inside the trigger guard. He opened fire too soon. With a stuttering SMG he drew a line of 9 mm holes across the front of the freezer, into the back of the open door and through the chest of his astonished partner. The string of Parabellums hammered the man into the door, and slammed the door into the unit's front wall. As the heart-shot thug bounced forward onto his face, the freezer door started to close.

Brognola got off two shots before the second cover guy could fire at him. The slugs hit the drug soldier in the chest and chin, bowling him over like a tenpin.

Brognola couldn't tell whether the wild shooter had hit the guy in the freezer or whether the guy was laying low for a moment to take stock of the situation. But he knew he had to keep the soldier from getting out of the freezer and coming at his back.

The big Fed hobbled across the kitchen and, as he did, he snatched up a sharpening steel from a slotted knife stand on a counter. He slammed the freezer door shut, fitted the tip of the steel into the hole in the handle, and slapped it down as far as it would go.

A second later, bullets started flying through the sheet metal from inside the freezer. Ragged holes appeared across its front wall. On the other side of the room, the tile shattered, as did the row of tall windows, which sent big chunks of glass sheeting down into the double sinks.

Diving for his life, Brognola threw himself to the ground and rolled away. The impact with the floor increased the pain in his leg, and when he got up, he was hobbling worse than ever. Tucking the pistol into his pocket, he scooped up a stubby submachine gun that had been dropped by one of the dead cartel thugs. He checked the fire selector switch to make sure it was set for full-auto and that the safety was off. Then he hopped through the doorway, back into the storeroom.

From the other side of the hacienda he could hear shouts. They were coming his way, and fast.

Brognola's heart sank when he realized he still wasn't going to make it to the door at the end of the room. The only cover between him and the door was a pallet of rice and beans in gunny sacks. A very low stack. And it was a long way from the pallet to the exit for a guy with only one good leg.

Once again he put his back to the storeroom wall. He heard the soft footsteps of the thugs as they advanced into the kitchen, his brain working at hyperspeed. The bodies of their crew were in plain sight. They would move close to check them for signs of life. They would see the sharpening steel stuck in the freezer's door handle, remove it and open the door.

Muffled gunfire from a single weapon ripped through the kitchen.

Then came an answering chorus, unmuffled.

Brognola realized at once that none of the shots were aimed at him. He poked his submachine gun around the corner. Two more Samosa soldiers were standing straight-legged, pouring full-automatic fire into the front of the freezer. Their roaring weapons spewed streams of spent hulls. A third soldier, mortally wounded in the chest and stomach, the sharpening steel still clutched in his hand, stumbled away from the partially opened door, shot by mistake by the guy in the freezer.

Brognola cut loose, sweeping automatic fire in a barely controlled arc across the kitchen. He started out aiming low, skimming slugs off the top of the butcher-block table, and ended up high, blasting a big clock off the far wall. In between, he stitched bullets through the two gunmen, making them twist into the floor.

When he stopped shooting, it got quiet again.

There was no sound inside the freezer.

He had bought himself a few minutes, at best. He hurled himself across the storeroom, heading for the door at the other end. Through the windowpanes in its upper half, he could see the neatly raked gravel of a courtyard. It had to be an exit.

He was still fifteen feet from the doorway when someone cursed behind him. Then gunfire boomed at his back. Heavy slugs sailed past his head and chewed chunks out of the facing door frame and wall, shattering the door's little windowpanes.

He wasn't going to make it.

Turning sideways, Brognola frantically hopped, then threw himself down behind the pallet of sacks. Bullets plucked at the bags of beans just above his head and loose beans cascaded down, skittering over the floor.

He'd lost the element of surprise. There was nothing to keep the drug soldiers from regrouping and overrunning him. He took the Smith out of his pocket and set it down on the ground in front of him. Then he gripped the SMG in both hands.

He had to return fire to keep them at bay.

Brognola popped up from behind the pile of sacks. He sprayed gunfire toward the storeroom entrance. As he did, he saw a dark shape, on each side of the doorway. The cartel soldiers ducked back as bullets flew their way. Figuring that the wall was no real cover from Parabellums, Brognola saturated it and both sides of the doorway.

After a second or two of pure, pulverizing rampage upon the Sheetrock, the Heckler & Koch locked back in Brognola's hand, empty. Through the haze of gunsmoke, he saw first one man topple across the threshold, then heard the thud of the other as he hit the floor on the other side of the holed-out wall.

Discarding the H&K and picking up the Smith, Brognola hauled himself up and lurched for the exit. Hopping into the sunlight, he was confronted by an enclosed yard, a tiny, private garden bordered by a high, solid, masonry wall.

The only direct access to the little courtyard was the doorway he'd come through. There was no gate leading out of the enclosure. The cook and his helpers were long gone. Brognola couldn't figure out how they'd done it, at first. Then he noticed the four-foot-tall ceramic pot standing against the opposite wall. It held a small fruit tree. Beside the slender trunk, on the putty-colored wall, he saw the pale print of a shoe. One of the tree limbs was broken, and bark was stripped from the trunk. The cook and his lady friends had climbed onto the pot, then used the tree trunk to help them reach the top of the wall.

In Brognola's condition that was impossible.

There was no cover in the garden for him to fight from behind. The only defense against bullets was the exterior wall of the hacienda. Brognola leaned his back against it. It was blistering hot from the sun.

Brognola dropped the Smith's magazine into his left hand and counted the live rounds through the slot in the side. He slapped the mag back into the pistol and let himself slide down the wall until his butt hit the ground. Standing was wasted effort.

He wasn't going anywhere.

He had eight shots left.

Eight shots between him and the Reaper.

UNDER THE HAIL of cartel lead, Mack Bolan ran uphill toward the muzzles of the high-ground automatic weapons. With tree bark, dust and slugs zooming past his head, the Executioner charged up the slope for all he was worth. He took a straight-line track through the scrub, clawing his way over the tangled vines and whippy limbs to save time. A zigzag route would have only given the opposition a wider window to shoot at him.

There was twenty feet of cleared ground between the row of houses and the edge of the trees. The route was steep. Bullets slapped the earth in front of him as a submachine gun fired down from the porch railing directly above. Grunting from the effort, legs driving, Bolan hurled himself forward under the shadow of the stilt-supported rear deck, out of the shooters' firing lanes. He rolled to his back, bringing the M-16 up to his shoulder. The porch was seventy-five feet above him.

The gunfire stopped for a moment, echoes fading into the hillside jungle, then the guy standing on the porch above him stepped over the rail. Hanging on with one hand, he squatted and pointed his weapon under the deck. The SMG clattered, spewing unaimed fire back and forth.

He was hoping for a lucky hit.

The gunman couldn't see Bolan, but Bolan could see him.

The Executioner acquired the target in the four-power scope and fired twice. The first shot hit the man in the hand, making him drop his weapon. The soldier put his second bullet through the underside of the porch's decking. He couldn't tell where he'd hit the guy, but the impact of the slug broke the man's grip on the railing and he fell, his arms and legs flailing, crashing into the scrub below. It got really quiet for a moment, so quiet that Bolan could hear the rustling as the body slid over the wet vegetation, down the slope.

Then a couple of the drug soldiers started yelling. "Do you see him? Where is he?" Bolan heard the voice of a third guy. It sounded like he had a walkie-talkie and was calling for help from the hacienda. Bolan didn't want to give them time to get organized.

That meant he had to make a momentary backtrack.

He sprinted underneath the line of porches until he found the one he was looking for. Using the M-16's scope, he scanned the underside of the deck. With its magnification at such close range, he could see the shadows of the soldiers' boots through the gaps in the planking.

The Executioner aimed between what had to be a pair of feet. The M-16 bucked into his shoulder as he sent a burst of gunfire ripping through the boards. The tight cluster of tumblers caught the cartel thug in the crotch, spearing into his guts. The soldier dropped to his knees, screaming.

Before the others could retreat from the deck to the safety of the house, Bolan cut loose again, emptying the 30-round clip. More chunks of wood blasted free as he sawed through the planks with a stream of hot lead. Caught in midstride, the drug soldiers took multiple hits to the legs and stomach.

Then the porch gave way.

The men dropped through the gap, screaming, pinwheeling to the ground. Bolan had to roll out of the way of the falling bodies and boards. When the soldiers hit, they made distinct snapping sounds, the sounds of breaking bones, and then they, too, slid on, disappearing into the slope's slick undergrowth.

After reloading with a fresh magazine from his pack, Bolan moved along the path that climbed toward the gated, private road that led to the hacienda. From his recon map, he knew that the entrance to the road at the village was protected by a guardhouse. The men on duty would have already been alerted by the ruckus he had caused. They had to know the fastest route up to the road was the path he was on.

They would be in position, waiting for him.

Anticipating a welcoming committee, Bolan broke off the trail and beat through the bush. When he reached the edge of the scrub, he dropped to his belly and crawled forward for a clear view.

Above him, 150 feet away, the two guards knelt on the shoulder of the road. They were silhouetted against the sky. One of them held a pair of binoculars and was scanning the terrain below, looking for the intruder.

The Executioner poked the barrel of the M-16 out of the brush and put the scope to this eye. His finger found the selector switch and he moved it into single-shot position. The firing angle was steeply upward. He locked onto his target, taking out the closest man first.

The rifle chugged into his shoulder as he snapped the trigger. A puff of red steam plumed from the top of the guard's head as the 5.56 mm round cored out the inside of his skull. Bolan rode the recoil onto the second target. He didn't have to swing the M-16 down very far to acquire it.

Seeing what had happened to his pal, the other guard jumped up and tried to turn away, to retreat from the road. Bolan hit him behind the left arm, just above his hip, and the shot angled up through his torso, coming out through the top of his right shoulder.

Like magic, the guard vanished from view.

Scrambling to his feet, Bolan climbed the last thirty feet to the road. As the recon map had indicated, there were no guardrails. On both sides of the pavement were sheer drop-offs.

The Executioner jogged down the road to where the two drug soldiers lay. The first guy was stone dead, the second was still conscious, eyes bugging out from the pain. The Executioner finished him with a mercy shot, then rolled both men off the edge of the road, letting them tumble into the dense brush.

Just as he'd moved the bodies off the shoulder, he heard the roar of engines coming from the direction of the hacienda compound. He immediately jumped down from the road onto the slope and lay flat, keeping his eyes just above the level of the pavement.

Two more of the cartel's Suburbans burst through a gate in the hacienda's front wall, throwing up a cloud of dust. The first vehicle swerved for a second as it hit the asphalt. All its windows were down, and he could see the heads of drug soldiers inside.

The Executioner rolled to his back and yanked a grenade off his combat harness. The SUVs were coming his way, fast. He pulled the pin with his teeth and let the safety lever flip off, priming it. When the first Suburban was three car lengths away, he pushed off the ground and neatly tossed the frag through the front passenger's window, onto the lap of a very surprised soldier.

The lead Suburban swerved again, brake lights flashing, and this time the swerving was more violent as both the driver and his passenger tried to pick the fused and smoking grenade off the floorboard.

It was a six-second fuse.

They ran out of time.

The Suburban jolted with a rocking boom, and orange

fire blossomed through the dust and splinters of the blown-out front and rear windows. For a fraction of a second the ball of flame turned the six human forms inside into black cutout shapes. The SUV continued its veering course, rolling off the road and barreling down the jungle's slopes, leaving a wake of snapped off and uprooted scrub trees.

The second Suburban's brakes locked an instant after the explosion, skidding in a wild arc that almost took it off the road, too. The vehicle came to a stop broadside to Bolan, fifty feet away. All its doors popped open at once.

Before the driver and his four passengers could bail out, the Executioner had dropped the M-16's selector switch to full and opened fire, stitching a line of holes across its partially open doors. Two men jerked under the waist-high stream of lead, slamming into the door frames, then sliding limply under the doors, onto the road.

The other three soldiers exited on the far side of the vehicle and returned fire over the Suburban's hood and roof. The concentrated autofire forced Bolan to step off the road for cover.

As he started to pop up again, slugs from below and behind him whacked the slope to his right. Survivors from the porches maybe, or reinforcements from the village square.

Either way, he was bracketed by hostile fire.

Bolan pushed up from the slope, scrambled over the top and sprinted across the road. The guys firing from behind the Suburban chewed up the asphalt at his heels. Before they could catch him in their sights, he dived off the other side of the road. He rolled and jumped up, dashing along the face of the slope, following the gentle curve of the road toward the hacienda's front wall.

Behind him there was shouting as the two groups of drug soldiers, the ones who'd chased him up the trail and those at the Suburban, joined forces. They were celebrating, but they weren't chasing him, yet. If they left the protection of the SUV, they would have to run straight into his fire.

Their hesitation gave Bolan just enough time to reach the hacienda. As he raced over the road heading for the open front gates, a barrage of gunfire came pelting down at him. The submachine guns of the hardmen at the SUV gnawed holes in the masonry wall over his head and in front of him, but he ducked through the gate without being struck.

He found himself in an inner courtyard parking area. As he once again reloaded the M-16, he surveyed the terrain. In the center of the courtyard was a circular stone fountain surrounded by concentric rings of flower beds. On the other side of the fountain was the front of the four-story hacienda. It had a long shaded porch and arched windows. The ground-level front doors stood wide open, perhaps left that way by the guys in the Suburbans.

As he crossed the compound, running fast and low, Bolan heard blistering gunfire coming from inside the building.

Brognola.

It had to be Brognola.

HAL BROGNOLA could hear the drug soldiers whispering in the kitchen. He couldn't understand what they were saying but he figured they were discussing how they should proceed next. They didn't know that Brognola was in way over his head. All they could see was the bloody aftermath of what he'd accomplished up to this point. There were nine dead cartel crew on the kitchen floor and no dead former prisoner. They knew he had a nail hole in the palm of his right hand but that didn't seem to interfere with his shooting. They didn't know that he had an injured ankle.

They didn't know he had less than half a clip of ammo left.

In the distance Brognola kept hearing the rattle of a running gunfight. He wasn't the only one playing havoc with Samosa's troops. The other battlefront seemed to be coming closer and closer. Then he heard the hard crack of an explosion that had to be from another hand grenade. From the sound of it, no more than five hundred yards away.

If Bolan was that close, there was still hope.

Brognola steeled himself. He wouldn't let his old friend down, wouldn't let him come so far, through so much danger, only to drag home a shot-up corpse.

Out of the corner of his eye, the big Fed caught movement atop the perimeter wall to his right. A shadowy form, popping up. At once, gunfire barked at Brognola from a downward angle.

He swung up the Smith, braced it against his good leg and fired once, a snap shot into the middle of the sun-silhouetted head and shoulders. The booming report of the 9 mm was followed a split second later by a wet slapping sound as the jacketed slug caught the guy high on the breastbone. It had to have clipped his spinal cord because the next instant, he was falling forward over the top of the wall, arms dangling loose, weapon slipping free. The shooter crumpled in a heap at the base of the wall.

So much for the sneak attack, Brognola thought. The guy probably climbed through the busted-out kitchen windows, trying to flank him and catch him off guard.

At a shout from inside the kitchen, the soldiers there rushed through the storeroom doorway.

Brognola took the lowest possible shooting position, popping out from around the foot of the door frame. With the side of his face practically resting on the ground, he sighted on the men running at him. A barrage of bullets turned the doorway into flying splinters and plaster dust, as he punched out answering single shots. He tried to keep count of the expended rounds as he pulled the trigger, but in the heat of battle it was tough.

Two of the drug soldiers twisted as they were hit and went down hard. The other three made it to cover. Before they could turn their concentrated fire on him, Brognola pulled back around the corner of the doorway.

Bullets clawed at the threshold where his head had just been.

Looking down, he saw that the Smith's action had locked back. He stared at the thick, white smoke curling from its barrel and ejection port. He could see the empty magazine's floor plate.

From inside the storeroom came a guttural cry, then the scrape of boots as the three surviving gunmen charged him.

Reaper time.

13

Sitting on the bridge's built-in couch, Admiral Oswaldo Fuentes got control of his outrage only with the utmost difficulty. It was difficult because he took the violation personally. His bridge, his command, his ship, his manhood had all suffered a catastrophic insult. But Fuentes knew there was more at stake than his own hurt pride. There was a loyal crew and a very expensive vessel, the safety of which was his ultimate responsibility.

Sitting on the couch, he cleared his mind. And did one of the things he did best.

Analyze, he told himself. Analyze.

Who were the men with guns?

Terrorists, of course. His first look at them told him that. But were their goals political? What use did they have for this ship? They couldn't steal the DIV and then hope to use its weaponry to attack some major coastal target. The moment the vessel was identified as missing, a massive search operation would begin. And when it was found, it would be surrounded by air and sea, by the full power of the United States military. Short of surrender, and far short of any strategic target, it would be blown out of the water. The men who had taken his ship had to know that the Americans wouldn't negotiate with them. They had to know that trying to hold the DIV for ransom would only get them killed.

It occurred to Fuentes that if the terrorists couldn't use

the weaponry and couldn't collect a ransom, all they could do with the *Bernardo Chinle* was destroy it. Putting two and two together, it suddenly became clear why they were headed at full speed to a spot along the Middle America Trench, the closest deep water off the coastal shelf.

Why the *Bernardo Chinle*? Admiral Fuentes realized that the DIV had to be a specific, intended target, not a general target of opportunity. Other ships at the Las Cruces yard were less well protected and much easier to steal. Clearly, not just any Mexican naval vessel would do for these terrorists' purposes. Which meant only one thing: they had to belong to or have been hired by a drug cartel, most likely the Samosa organization. Their mission's object was to end the DIV program, which threatened the cartel's lifeblood, by sinking its prototype.

Fuentes put himself in the terrorists' position. If he were in charge, would he set the crew adrift in lifeboats before he sank the ship? A crew that could explain what had happened and who was responsible wasn't going to help the cartel's cause. Such information would focus attention and anger, and bring down even more concentrated heat from the United States. If Fuentes was in charge, he knew he would make sure the crew went down with the ship. There would be no survivors, except for the squad of terrorist gunmen. The ship's loss would then be a mystery, something that required months of investigation, something that could be used as a political football. Any elected official who insisted on proceeding with the program would be tarred with the loss of the *Bernardo Chinle*.

The admiral counted eight terrorists. It was infuriating to him that so few enemy had been able to seize control of the ship. His men weren't prepared for an attack. No one had foreseen the possibility. The sailors weren't even armed. Playing back his mental tape of earlier events, Fuentes discounted the idea that the gunmen had come on board in the minutes immediately after the launch, while the ship was still moored to the pier. There were too many eyes watching the DIV from all angles. Not just the sailors securing the lines, but the men standing in formation on the dock, waiting to board, and the dignitaries in the viewing stand.

No, there was only one opportunity for the terrorists to get on board, and that was during the brief grounding of the ship on the sandbar.

The admiral stared at the small, round bald spot on the back of Trevor Eames's head. Under the fringe of sandy-blond hair, his scalp was bright pink. What had seemed like an unfortunate, but minor, accident, now appeared much more ominous.

Fuentes had always thought the American a bit stiff and formal, but had put that reserve down to his British heritage. Eames had always been a devoted worker, apparently committed to the project body and soul. Many times he had logged in eighteen or twenty hours straight, trying to bring the computer system up to speed in order to make the launch deadline. Fuentes had never dreamed that the man would betray him and the ship to the cartel.

If that betrayal was real, the leader of the terrorists certainly hadn't given it away, yet. He paced the bridge, seeming to hardly notice Eames, addressing him only when he wanted specific information or to issue specific commands. Keeping the expat Briton's role secret would insure that if by accident a survivor or two escaped, no one could confirm his role in the theft and mass murder.

Fuentes studied the terrorist leader closely. From the man's air of command, it was obvious that he'd had formal military training. The admiral sensed no deference from the man to his own rank. Instead he radiated a blatant, bristling contempt. And he had shot poor Elizondo like a stray dog. It all made Fuentes think the man was neither a naval officer nor a Mexican. He was clearly Latin American, though.

Watching the terrorist's eyes, the way he kept control of his men, the admiral had no doubt that any attempt by the bridge crew to rush the pirates would fail.

The only way Fuentes was going to retake his bridge and rescue his locked-down crew was with outside support. But no one knew they were even in trouble. Their going off radar wouldn't draw immediate suspicion from anyone, and it certainly wouldn't initiate a search op. It would simply be seen as part of the sea trials, a test of the system.

Somehow, he had to get off a radio signal, but the bridge's communication had been shut down. There wasn't even a receiver up and running. And even if it had been up, there was no way the terrorists would allow a distress message to be transmitted.

The admiral let himself sink back into the couch.

After a moment, an answer came to him. It wasn't perfect, but it was all he could think of.

The *Bernardo Chinle* was equipped with automatically deployable EPIRBs. Emergency Position Indicating, Radio-transmitting Beacons. The floating beacons were meant to be used during active pursuit of drug suspects to mark ditched shipments of contraband for pickup after the smuggling suspects were in custody. The chances were good that the terrorists would never see the small flame-orange canister with antennae, bobbing in the ship's wake. The seawater-activated radio transmitter would tell the world that something had happened to the *Bernardo Chinle,* something out of the ordinary. They weren't supposed to be chasing drug runners, yet. This was just a shakedown cruise to test the ship's seaworthiness. The transmitter beacon, if deployed near enough to their final destination, would lead help right to them.

Fuentes shut his eyes and tried to visualize the keypad

sequence for the remote deployment of an EPIRB. How many finger strokes did it take to pull up the correct command window? Ten? Twelve? Once the window was up on the screen, a double tap on the launch icon would deploy the device, then another double tap and the window was gone. It would be over in four seconds, max.

Could the crewman do it all without being noticed by the terrorists?

Could the admiral somehow communicate what he wanted done, and when?

From where Fuentes sat, the navigation screen was visible, as was the constantly adjusted ETA. He had exactly forty-three minutes to get his point across.

14

Hacienda Corto de Vista

Mack Bolan charged through the open double front doors in a flat-out sprint. As he leapt over the threshold, he came toe-to-toe with two cartel gunmen who were running out of the building. Big, dark blurs.

There wasn't time for thought, for putting on the brakes or swerving to one side to avoid a head-on collision. There was only time for an instinctive, instantaneous and violent reaction.

And the Executioner had the decided edge in that department.

Swiveling his torso, Bolan brought the M-16's butt around in a tight arc. He clipped the hardman on the right across the chin with the gun butt. And following through with the twisting movement, shoulder-butted the other oncoming gunman in the middle of the chest.

The first guy's lights winked out, maybe forever. His neck made a crisp snapping sound as the powerful blow to his jaw drove his chin over his right shoulder. Way over his shoulder. His legs went to mush and he fell forward, dropping his weapon before landing limply sprawled across the floor.

The other full-charging thug met an immovable object. He bounced back from the Executioner's solid shoulder strike, doubling up as his rib cage fractured and the breath was knocked out of him. The drug soldier dropped to the floor on his back, gasping for air.

Bolan pressed the M-16's flash hider against the middle of his breastbone and fired once. Flesh and bone muffled the 5.56 mm bullet's crack. The gunner's arms and legs jerked violently at the impact, and his torso lifted off the floor in a sudden, all-out, death-throe convulsion.

The Executioner hopped the spreading crimson puddle and advanced, scanning the upper-floor balconies for signs of movement. Though he checked all sides, there were no opposition in evidence. The sounds of gunfire that had drawn him into the hacienda had stopped. It was eerily quiet.

If Brognola was still alive, if the last exchange hadn't finished him, he could have been anywhere in the big house.

Bolan noticed a pair of boots sticking out from behind a sideboard. He moved along the cover of the first-floor balcony's overhang, approaching quickly, with M-16 ready in his fist. The hardman lying on his chest wasn't ever going to get up again. He'd tried to use the sideboard as cover.

Bullets had ripped big chunks out of the thin plywood veneer that covered the back of the piece of furniture, catching him multiple times in the neck and side. From the looks of it, he had bled to death where he lay. He'd probably never felt it, though. His spinal cord had been severed at the base of his skull.

A few feet farther, in front of the hacienda's huge fireplace, another drug soldier lay facedown, arms and legs spread wide. Kneeling, Bolan saw that the hole in his back wasn't round. The bullet that had killed him had gone through his back sideways, ripping through the organs in his chest.

Another volley of automatic weapon fire erupted from

the other side of the house. Which meant Brognola was still alive.

Bolan broke into a run, following the waves of auto-bursts out of the main room, down the short corridor to the kitchen.

Before he even rounded the doorway, he caught the concentrated stench of blood. Lots and lots of blood. It smelled like a slaughterhouse. He entered the kitchen low and fast.

Right away, he saw the tangled bodies strewed along the left side of the room. Heads shot to pieces, chests turned inside out by close-range gunfire. The front of the freezer unit was stitched with exit and entry bullet holes. Around the room, the white tile was likewise riddled with holes and the windows over the sink had been completely shot out.

Brognola had unleashed pure, living hellfire in the white room. He had made the cartel bastards pay dearly.

And the paying wasn't over, yet.

A tightly spaced string of 9 mm single shots whined out of the doorway directly ahead of Bolan, slamming into the tile wall to his right, sending bits of white shrapnel flying around the room. A second later, the walls shook as auto-,fire answered the single shots in a withering stream.

As the Executioner beelined for the storeroom door, the gunfire suddenly stopped. He was still three running strides from the threshold, when he heard a shout from the room ahead.

It was a call to break cover, to charge and overrun the opposition.

Bolan raced through the storeroom doorway as the first drug soldier reached the exit on the other side of the room. Two others moved right on the first guy's heels. The Executioner fired from the hip as he ran, stitching the lead guy with full-metal jacket slugs that spun him sideways, shoulder-first into the doorjamb. His knees buckled and he fell backward across the doorway. Keeping the M-16's trigger pinned, Bolan walked bullets across the second gunner's back, sending him first staggering to his knees, then down onto his stomach.

Though Bolan held the trigger pinned, his weapon stopped firing. The M-16's action had jammed.

Meanwhile, the third drug soldier managed to put on the brakes, and spun to face the attack from the rear. As he did so, he brought his submachine gun up in both hands.

Bolan flipped the M-16's charging handle, clearing the stuck round with a snap of the wrist. Before the ejected cartridge hit the floor, both gun muzzles had locked on their respective targets.

Twelve feet separated the gun sights.

The face-off that followed only lasted a fraction of a second.

In the other man's dark, clouded eyes, under the fury and the excitement of a full-on to-the-death confrontation, Bolan glimpsed a tiny flicker of fear, a spark that blossomed, then spread.

In the Executioner's eyes the drug soldier saw the blue of the glacier's deep crevasse. He felt the chill of a marble mortuary slab pressed against his bare back.

The man's fear first made him slow.

Then it killed him.

The Executioner hip-fired four rounds. Two rounds into it, already shot though both lungs, staggering, eyes squeezed shut, blood fountaining from his mouth, the Samosa soldier pinned his own weapon's trigger. The SMG in his hands clattered, raking the air, spewing a stream of spent brass, cutting zigzags in the tile wall on the other side of the room.

Bolan's last two shots caught the soldier as he dropped,

plowing through the bridge of his nose and the center of his forehead. The gunner slumped to the floor.

"Hal! Hal, you out there?" the Executioner shouted at the open doorway, which was now jammed with still-twitching bodies.

"Yeah, I'm here," came the reply from a very familiar voice. "I could use some help."

Bolan stepped over the corpses and out the door. His old friend sat propped against the exterior wall. He looked like death warmed over. His unshaven face was ashen and drawn, his clothes were ripped and stained with blood. His right hand was a real mess. One glance at it and Bolan knew what had happened.

He knelt to get a better look at the damage. "Ramon Murillo?" he asked.

"Yeah," Brognola answered, "and the sick bastard would've pounded the other two nails in me if Yovana's boys hadn't sneaked in and given me a hacksaw. Those kids saved my life, Striker. They flat-out saved my life. And what they did cost Ramon Murillo his."

"A couple of real brave kids," the Executioner said, nodding. This was something he knew from experience.

What he didn't know was who their real father was.

When Brognola dropped the bombshell, Bolan's face showed no emotion whatsoever. Inwardly, however, his stomach twisted and tightened into a hard knot.

"Do you think he's still here?" the Executioner said.

"He left in his helicopter."

"Yeah, I saw it go."

"I know he took the boys with him. They don't deserve the father they've got. Life can be a real bitch sometimes."

That was the height of understatement as far as Bolan was concerned. "Let's get you up on your feet," he said.

"Not easily done, Striker. My ankle is badly twisted. Christ, it might even be broken."

Bolan lifted Brognola's trouser cuff. Even so, he could see there was no way the shoe was coming off; the foot and ankle were too swollen. And there was no time to deal with that now.

"Are you shot?"

"No, thank God," the big Fed said. "I lucked out in that department." Brognola took a breath, grimaced, then said, "I saw Samosa face-to-face. He told me something, figuring I'd take it to my grave. The cartel is going to steal the prototype DIV this morning. For all I know, they may have already taken it."

"What are they going to do with it?"

"They plan to take it out into blue water and sink it with all hands. We can't let that happen, Striker. The campaign against the cartel depends on state-of-the-art interdiction ships strangling the smugglers' sea routes. We've can't let that happen. We've got to stop them."

"First things first, Hal," Bolan said as he dumped the M-16's spent magazine and cracked in a fresh one from his backpack. "We've got to get clear of this building and away from the village. I left a bunch of live Samosa gunmen on the road leading up to the hacienda. They will have regrouped by now. Our best bet is to take the hillside down through the jungle. But we're going to have to fight our way out."

"I'm up for it. Give me a hand."

Bolan helped Brognola back into the storeroom. He let his friend rest against a tier of shelves for a moment while he scavenged a rag-head mop that was lying on the floor in a corner. He broke the handle over his knee, then handed the makeshift crutch to Brognola. "If it's the right length it should make moving around a little easier for you," he said.

Brognola slid the mop head under his arm. "Perfect," he said.

The Executioner picked up one of the dead soldiers' submachine guns from the floor, checked its magazine, then gave it to the Fed. He stripped the magazines out of two other dropped autoweapons and Brognola put them in his pants pockets.

With Bolan on point, and Brognola hobbling along behind on the broken mop, they hurried as fast as they could back through the hacienda. When they reached the front doors, Bolan took a quick look out, checking the courtyard over the sights of his M-16.

"We're clear all the way to the front wall," he said as he drew back. "Wait until I make the fountain, then come after me."

The Executioner ducked out from under the hacienda's long porch roof, cut across the open ground to the flower beds, where he dropped to one knee. He stuck his head up over the rim of the fountain. Because of the angle of view, he could only see partway down the road.

Clear.

Waving Brognola on, he skirted the perimeter of the fountain and ran for the high exterior wall, keeping out of the line of fire from the road. With his back flat to the wall, the Executioner watched his friend struggle to the fountain, then limp across the gravel to the wall beside him.

Brognola's face was swathed in sweat, but it had lost some of its ashen, shocked color, which Bolan took as a good sign. From outside the compound, he heard the sound of a vehicle starting up. The engine got louder and louder. It was coming their way.

A very bad sign.

The Executioner dropped to his side and peered around the foot of the wall at the open gate. He drew back at once.

"What is it?" Brognola said.

"I left an SUV intact on the access road," Bolan told him. "I shot it up pretty good but didn't kill it. I was in a hurry to get to you. I should've killed it. It's moving up the road at a dead crawl with about a dozen guys behind it. They're using it for rolling cover."

"What can we do?"

"Try to keep them off us."

With that, the Executioner dived across the open gateway to the other side of the wall. A second after he reached safety, a volley of automatic weapon fire ripped through the entrance, chipping at the fountain's rim, gouging furrows in the parking area's gravel.

"Stay low," Bolan told him. "Fire in short bursts and aim for the SUV's driver or the front end."

"Gotcha."

"On the count of three, then," the Executioner said. "One, two, three—"

Bolan popped out from around the bottom of the gate, showing only half his head and the tip of his shoulder to the rolling vehicle some hundred yards away. He fired the M-16 left-handed in full-auto mode, punching a tight ring of bullet holes through the Suburban's windshield. Brognola swung out and fired, too, but his aim was less accurate. His bullets trammeled the hood and the top of the left fender.

Return fire drove them back behind the wall almost at once.

The SUV kept rolling, but its horn sounded.

And kept on sounding.

Until the other drug soldiers pulled the dead guy off the steering wheel.

"If we stop the car, Striker," the big Fed said, "we're still screwed. They can still shoot from behind it. And keep us trapped in here."

"If we don't," the soldier told him, "we've got no chance. Zero. Ready to go again? One, two, three—"

When the Executioner swung out again, he was standing upright. This time he aimed for the Suburban's front grille. In a single, blistering burst, he put seven holes in the radiator, then he ducked back behind the wall. Brognola's burst went wide a second time, but it took out one of the soldiers standing on the left side of the SUV. The gunman fell onto the shoulder of the road, dropping his weapon as he did so. He didn't move again.

The Suburban kept coming. The hail of autofire peppering the outside of the wall pulverized it and turned it into dust.

Then came the sound of an engine chugging, stalling, dying. The starter whined, clattered, but the motor refused to turn over.

Bolan took a quick look around the gate. He wasn't surprised to see the Suburban was still moving. The eight surviving soldiers were pushing the heavy vehicle ahead of them. If there was anybody driving, he was hiding below the dashboard.

The Executioner jerked a fragmentation grenade from his combat harness, primed it and, stepping back away from the wall, chucked it as far as he could in the direction of the SUV.

The hard crack of detonation echoed off the surrounding hills.

A look around the gate told Bolan his throw was short. There was a scorched place in the middle of the road, and a cloud of gray smoke hanging over it.

The SUV had stopped, just beyond the range of Bolan's arm. The drug soldiers hiding behind it continued to pepper the gateway, though they had switched to single shots, to conserve their ammunition.

"Go on without me, Striker," Brognola said. "I'm the

one who's keeping you from making a break for it. Face facts, I can't make it down the hill on this crutch even where the grade isn't so steep. Hell, I can hardly walk on flat ground. You've got to let them know about the DIV.''

Bolan didn't answer.

"I'll cover you, Striker," Brognola said. "Go on, beat it off the road, down the slope while you still can. Sooner or later they'll send a few guys to circle behind us. They're probably doing it right now."

"Your suggestion is not acceptable, my friend," Bolan said. "We're leaving together or we're not going anywhere."

"I appreciate the sentiment, but you're not thinking straight—"

"Shut up," Bolan said. "Listen..."

Off in the distance, they could hear the steady, throbbing beat of a helicopter.

"That way," the Executioner said, pointing at the sky to the north.

When the chopper appeared, it came over the hilltops out of the blinding sun, and it was impossible to even tell its color. But for sure, it was swooping down on the hacienda.

From the silhouette, Bolan identified it. "Blackhawk," he told Brognola.

"Ours or theirs?"

Considering the breadth and depth of the Samosa payroll, the answer to that question could have gone either way.

"Get down and stay down," Bolan said as he shouldered the M-16. "If they shoot at us, we shoot back."

The helicopter appeared over the top of the hacienda, its engines howling, a green blur sweeping over the courtyard, turning the fountain's spray to fine mist, whipping up clouds of stinging dust from the gravel.

It was past them in the blink of an eye, scooting over the front wall and down the road.

Bolan stuck his head around the gate in time to see the Blackhawk fire three air-to-ground rockets then peel off to the right, over the edge of the cliff. The Suburban exploded in a coruscating ball of fire. Its sheet-metal parts, hood, fenders and doors spiraled off into space.

"Guess it's ours!" Brognola shouted.

"Stay behind the wall," Bolan warned him as the chopper circled back toward them for another pass.

Not the whoosh of rockets this time, but the thunder of the Blackhawk's cargo bay–mounted, electrically driven cannon. A hellfire of shells pounded the road. Stray 20 mm, explosive-tipped rounds shot through the gate and skipped into the hacienda, sawing through the porch supports and dropping the roof and its load of orange tiles in a cloud of dust.

The cannon fire continued to rage at fifteen hundred rounds per minute, but the angle of attack shifted.

Brognola and Bolan both looked out to see the helicopter hovering over the burning SUV, the wash of its rotor flattening the flames, mixing black, oily smoke and flying debris. The Blackhawk's side gunner was methodically using his weapon's horrendous rate of fire to chew the dead bodies of the cartel soldiers into even smaller—and less recognizably human—pieces.

"Talk about overkill!" the big Fed cried as Bolan crossed over to his side of the gate. "They're not leaving anything big enough to bury."

"That's one of the reasons I came in after you by myself," the Executioner said. "Our Mexican counterparts aren't known for their restraint in hostage-type situations. They would have gotten you killed for sure, and probably with friendly fire."

"Who called them in?"

"The White House must've used up some big favors to give us an escape route and do the mopping up."

When the cannon fire finally stopped, the helicopter moved back from the flames and landed on the road, between the demolished SUV and the hacienda's front gate. A man in camo fatigues hopped out of the copilot's door and ran under the still-spinning rotor blade toward them, carrying an H&K G-3 assault rifle.

"I think we'd better toss our guns out on the road," Bolan said to Brognola. "We don't want our new friends to mistake us for a pair of drug-cartel goons." With that, he carefully laid down his rifle and Beretta 93-R in plain sight of the helicopter.

"Good idea," Brognola said, following Bolan's lead and chucking his commandeered submachine gun down beside the other weapons.

"Sirs," the Mexican marine lieutenant said as they stepped out from the gate with their hands in the air, "please, this isn't necessary. I'm glad to see you are still alive. We're your ride home."

With the young Mexican's help, Bolan assisted Brognola to the Blackhawk's side bay doors. Inside were four more marines. They got Brognola belted into a jump seat in the cargo bay.

"My friend needs to get to a hospital," Bolan said into the lieutenant's ear. "And I need a direct line to your commander."

"No problem. We're fifteen minutes away from our base hospital. There's a headset and microphone above your seat."

As the lieutenant gave orders to the pilot, the Executioner took a place beside Brognola. "We're getting you to a doc, right away," he said.

Hal nodded. "Thanks for coming for me."

"My pleasure," Bolan said. He put on the headset as the Blackhawk lifted off the road.

The lieutenant's voice crackled at him through the earphones. "We have one more thing to do," he said. "It will only take a minute...."

The Blackhawk banked at an extreme angle and swung around to look down on the hacienda again. Without fanfare, or warning, five more air-to-ground rockets whooshed from under the helicopter's belly and shot in a tight cluster toward the building.

They bored through the tile roof and buried themselves deep inside. A heartbeat later, the roof lifted upward, mushrooming with a tremendous roar. All the windows blew out. Then the exterior walls of the top story buckled and caved inward, taking most of the third story with them.

Fire licked up from the ruin as they banked again and started flying toward Mazatlán. When Bolan had his radio link to the marine commander a minute or two later, he told the officer in terse Spanish about the cartel's threat to seize the *Bernardo Chinle*.

Seeing the Executioner's expression suddenly change, Brognola leaned closer and asked him, "What's wrong?"

Bolan covered the microphone with the palm of his hand. "Bad news," he said into his old friend's ear. "The DIV fell off radar ten minutes ago."

15

The *Bernardo Chinle*'s ETA at the deepwater coordinates was down to five minutes and change when the sailor manning the sonar and fire control flat panels finally turned in his chair and looked over at his commanding officer. Fuentes caught his eye and held it. Very carefully, the admiral mouthed a word, that wasn't really a word at all. It was an acronym.

"EPIRB," Fuentes mimed.

The sailor frowned. He understood that something important was being relayed, but he hadn't grasped the gist of it.

Fuentes glanced around to make sure none of the terrorists were paying attention to him, then he repeated the silent command in an even more exaggerated and drawn out way.

The man's eyes lighted up. Message received.

Fuentes gave him the briefest of hand signals, a telegraphic movement indicating not yet, wait. Wait until I say so.

The sailor nodded minutely and turned back to his screens.

Thanks to its superstructure's unique shape and materials, and its complement of electronic hardware, the *Bernardo Chinle* had already vanished from land- and air-based radar. It had fallen off the world. The DIV was about to reappear in another form. The EPIRB, or Emergency

Position Indicating, Radio-transmitting Beacon, would send a homing signal when set adrift containing encrypted information, including the name of vessel, the time and nature of deployment, whether the ship was involved in a life-threatening situation, as in man overboard, or a pursuit operation. Although the long distance radio signal would give air and sea search and rescue teams something to home in on, there was no way to indicate to them what exactly had gone wrong—piracy wasn't part of any of the vessel's contingency plans. The rescue teams would have to figure out the situation when they arrived on scene, and hopefully before the terrorists activated the ship's ground-to-air missile defense system.

Fuentes had to give cover to the sailor at the sonar desk, to distract the attention of the terrorists while he executed the keypad commands to remote-deploy the EPIRB device. The admiral stared at the blood spatters on the bridge's wall and the bullet-cracked window from Elizondo's brutal and senseless murder. He knew all too well the risk he was taking. He thought about his young wife, Luisa, and he was glad he had kissed her goodbye.

The admiral pushed up from the couch.

All eyes turned toward him, standing there, huge and defiant.

Eyes and gun barrels.

The terrorist leader immediately rushed up and confronted him, with the raised H&K MP-5. "Didn't I warn you not to move?" he said angrily, reaching out and prodding the admiral so hard in the chest with the gun muzzle that it drove the man back a half step.

"Set my crew adrift in the lifeboats," Fuentes told him. "You don't need them for anything. And there's no reason for them to come to harm as a result of all this. If you need a hostage, I'll stay behind."

"You're not in charge here anymore," the leader said.

"I am, and I didn't ask for volunteers, or martyrs. Now, sit down and shut up or I'm going to kill you."

Fuentes gave the sailor at the sonar array an almost imperceptible nod.

Almost.

When the terrorist leader half turned and glanced over his shoulder to see who he was nodding at, Fuentes made a left-handed grab for the MP-5. His fingers closed on the front sight and stump of the muzzle. Using all of his body weight, Fuentes savagely twisted the weapon to the side, away from his chest, and let loose a right cross at the smaller man's face.

The jolt of contact, knuckles on chin, made the admiral's arm go numb all the way up to the elbow for an instant. The terrorist leader's head snapped to the side, his eyelids half closed, his eyes momentarily unfocused. As blood oozed over his front teeth, full consciousness returned. And he smiled, menacingly.

Fuentes swung at him again, only this time the guy ducked and the blow glanced relatively harmlessly off the side of his head.

The terrorist retaliated by kneecapping him with a heel kick.

Something cracked inside the admiral's knee and he staggered backward with a groan.

The leader sent the Heckler & Koch MP-5 crashing down on top of the admiral's head. Fuentes tried to protect himself with his hands, but the first blow had cut him badly. Blood poured from a three-inch scalp wound.

Grunting with the effort, the terrorist battered the defenseless admiral for a full minute, alternating flurries of kicks to the torso with slashing blows of the SMG. Gradually, under the barrage of hard strikes, Fuentes lost his balance and slumped to the deck, his back pressed against the bridge's wall. Blood drooled off the edge of his jaw and onto the front of his white shirt, over the rows of medals above his pocket.

When the terrorist finally broke off the attack, gasping for breath, Fuentes wiped dazedly at his chin with the back of his hand, smearing crimson over his cheek.

When he'd recovered, the leader shoved the gun between the admiral's lips. "Now, you either get on that seat and stay there, or I'm going to splatter your brains all over the wall."

Fuentes waved a hand weakly in surrender. He'd had enough, more than enough. He turned and pulled himself, hand over hand, back up on the bridge's couch.

As he slumped against the cushion, the sailor at the sonar fire control desk looked at him in amazement. In order to save the lives of the men under his command, the admiral had suffered a terrible beating.

The seaman then gave Fuentes a single, curt nod of the head that made all the pain worthwhile. The nod said, EPIRB away.

16

"Is that your new boat, Papa?" little Pedro exclaimed as the Sikorsky circled the slowly drifting DIV. "It has so many guns!"

Samosa was encouraged by the boy's show of interest. It was the first real enthusiasm he'd displayed since they'd left the hacienda. Perhaps, as the Don had hoped, the DIV would draw both of the boys out of their shells. "That is a very powerful warship, son," he said. "It could shoot down this helicopter from a distance of twenty miles. We couldn't even see the ship and it could still knock us out of the air."

"It's not going to shoot at us, is it?" Juanito said warily.

"No, of course not. It's perfectly safe. I control it."

"You bought a warship?" Juanito seemed somewhat astonished at the prospect.

"I paid for it, yes. And now I will show it to you." He gestured for the pilot to set down on the landing deck. "A little later I have a surprise for you. I think you'll enjoy it."

"Are you going to shoot off the guns?" Pedro said, wide-eyed.

For all his reserve, even Juanito was excited by the idea. "Tell us, Papa," he said. "Please…"

Samosa shook his head. "You'll have to wait and see, but you won't be disappointed."

After the pilot set the Sikorsky down on the pad, Ignacio

Nuñez and two of his men crossed the deck and opened the rear door for Samosa. He and the children piled out, then followed the Panamanians off the landing pad, through the telescoping hangar.

As they started down the two flights of steps leading to the main deck, the drug lord said, "Is everything going according to plan?"

"Yes, Don Jorge," Nuñez said over his shoulder. "We're just waiting for the Hatteras to arrive with the C-4." The SEAL leader paused at the first landing and pointed at a white speck bobbing on the horizon line. "That's it coming over there. It should be here in a few minutes."

Satisfied, Samosa nodded. "Come on, boys," he said, "let's have a look at the bridge."

He escorted his children along the starboard side of the ship, between the superstructure and the outside rail.

"Papa, there's no people on board," Juanito said. "Why is that? Isn't there a crew on board?"

"They're all taking a rest below deck," Nuñez told him. "It's their siesta time."

The boy seemed to accept this absurd answer for the time being, or perhaps he was merely distracted as they started climbing the steep metal stairs to the bridge.

Inside the *Bernardo Chinle*'s control room, four more Panamanian SEALs held the bridge staff at gunpoint. One of the prisoners had taken some punishment. A heavyset man with lots of medals on his chest and gold braid on his shoulders had a bloody face, a blood-drenched uniform shirt and one eye completely swollen shut.

Juanito visibly flinched at the sight of him. Then the boy pointedly looked away.

This reaction upset Samosa deeply. To survive, to thrive his boys needed to be immune to the suffering of others. There had to be clear boundaries between their own pain and the pain they caused. It was high time for a hardening of their hearts.

"This," the drug lord said, gesturing at the admiral, "is the former owner of this ship. He has most kindly delivered it to me."

"Why is he all bloody?" Juanito asked, numbly.

"He had an accident," Nuñez answered. "He wasn't paying attention and he got hurt."

"Can we play video games, Papa?" Pedro said, looking around at all the computer screens.

Juanito stared out the bridge's cracked front window.

Samosa knew that his sons were neither dim-witted nor naive. They both knew what had happened here, that their father had taken the ship by force. They were retreating into their respective shells again. Pedro by pretending nothing whatsoever had happened, that everything was perfectly normal; Juanito by glazing over. It was the opposite of the drug lord's intent. He wanted his boys involved in what was really happening on the ship. He wanted them to take part in the destruction, and to enjoy it. He wanted to undo what their mother had done to them, to unravel the concept of conscience she had woven into their self-images.

"I've got a better idea," the drug lord said. "Have you ever seen a great big ship like this sink?"

"You mean on TV?" Pedro said.

"No, for real."

"Who's going to sink the ship?" Juanito asked.

"We are."

"Why, Papa?" Pedro said.

"Because I want to," Samosa replied.

"Aren't we going to shoot off the guns?" Pedro asked. Samosa shook his head.

"You just bought the boat and now you're going to sink it?" Juanito said, somewhat puzzled.

"That is the power of money, son. Because I have so much of it I can do whatever I want. Nothing can stop me. Not the fat man there with the bloody face. Not all those big guns out on the deck or those brand-new computers. This ship is mine—ours—to destroy. I bought it so the three of us could watch it sink to the bottom of the sea."

Ignacio Nuñez turned from the bridge's side window. "Don Jorge," he said, "the Hatteras is pulling up alongside."

"Get down there and set your charges," Samosa told him. "I want to be in the air in twenty minutes with my boys, watching the show."

IGNACIO NUÑEZ left the bridge on the double. Right behind him were his two top explosives men, Salvator and Raimundo. They ran back along the ship's starboard side, to the superstructure wall that supported the flight deck. Over the rail below them, a man on the bow pulpit of the forty-two-foot sport fishing boat was tying a mooring line to the foot of the accommodation ladder. His submachine gun hung on a shoulder sling, barrel down.

On the Hatteras's flybridge, a man in sunglasses with silver hair, dressed in expensive casual clothes, waved up at Nuñez. "Hello, my friend!" shouted a beaming Joseph Crecca.

Nuñez knew him as one of Samosa's chief underbosses, a man with the power of life and death.

The Panamanian waved back.

Crecca descended the stainless steel ladder to the sport fisher's deck. As he did, five men stepped out from the boat's salon. To Nuñez they looked like Mexican bone-breakers. They weren't dressed for a sea voyage. They were all wearing cheap, gray suits. The underboss barked an order to them, then crossed over onto the DIV's accommodation ladder and started up.

The cartel thugs each retrieved a single, wax-coated, olive drab cardboard box from the low stack on the fantail, and carried it across the fishing vessel's gunwale to the foot of the ladder.

Nuñez didn't care for Crecca. From what Nuñez knew, Crecca was some kind of Croatian or Serbian, maybe a Yugoslavian, but he'd lived in Central America, and mostly Mexico, for decades.

"Don Jorge is impatient to have the thing over and done with. We're ready to lay the charges. Have your men bring the explosives along," Nuñez said.

After receiving the C-4, the three Panamanians headed toward the stairway leading belowdecks. Crecca didn't follow them down. Afraid to get grease on his baggy, tan silk pants, he continued toward the bridge.

Nuñez descended the stairs first. It was two flights down to the engine room. He didn't stop there to place a charge in the aft section of the ship. That wasn't part of the demolition plan. Instead, he continued down the narrow hallway. When he reached the middle of the DIV, he took another stairway down. It ran behind the ship's main cargo holds. At the bottom of the stairway was the watertight access door to the forward bilges.

Thanks to the American traitor, Eames, Nuñez had been able to supply an outside expert in naval demolition with copies of the actual architect's drawings of the DIV. After examining them, the demolition consultant had decided that the best way to send the ship down in one piece was to crack the hull right down the middle, from the inside out. All of the plastic explosive charges would be set along the forward part of the vessel's keel, at specific points marked on the structural drawings that Nuñez carried with him for reference.

It was a precision job that required strict attention to detail, and no shortcuts. Which was why it hadn't been left to the pack mules who lugged the boxes of C-4. The Mexicans could no more read a blueprint than he could play a slide trombone.

Nuñez unsealed the watertight door, hit the switch that controlled the interior floodlights, and entered the crawl space. Checking his map, he located the first placement site. He quickly marked the spot with a squirt of Day-Glo orange spray paint, then moved on.

Behind him, Salvator and Raimundo worked as a team. They opened one of the boxes, took the plastic explosive from its wrapper, cut a chunk of C-4 to size, and then armed it with a detonator cap and a radio-controlled remote activation switch. When they were done, they advanced to the next Day-Glo orange mark. The Mexican mules followed holding the boxes, obviously not happy that the oily bilge water and sharp steel edges all around were turning their cheap suits into stained rags.

Salvator and Raimundo spaced the charges at uneven intervals over a distance of sixty feet, according to the diagram. Each package of explosive was fitted with a blasting cap and a remote detonator switch.

When all the boxes were empty, and all the charges set to blow, Nuñez led them out of the bilges and back up the stairs to the main deck. There, he divided the crew into teams of three, each with a Panamanian for a leader.

"Now we go over the ship, deck by deck and room by room," he told them all. "This is important. The job has to be done right. I want every door and porthole sealed tight. Nothing, I repeat, nothing is supposed to float up to the surface after this ship goes down. If something does pop up, if it's found, it could tell the search parties where to concentrate their efforts. They'll bring in side-scanning sonar and drone submersibles with underwater cameras. Who knows? They might even get lucky and find it.

"The point is," Nuñez continued, "without debris to

work from, the searchers won't know where to start looking. The only thing they've got to go on is this ship's top speed. Based on that, the wreck site could be anywhere on hundreds of square miles of ocean floor. And that's how Don Jorge wants to keep it.''

17

When the Blackhawk touched down at the naval base just north of the Las Cruces shipyard, it was met by a military ambulance. A pair of uniformed paramedics waited beside a collapsible gurney. Bolan helped Brognola to ease out of the cargo bay. The attendants then moved him onto the gurney.

Brognola looked at Bolan and said, "I wish to hell I could come along with you, Striker. This is one job I'd like to see through to the bitter end."

"You've done enough," the Executioner told him. "You've been through enough. It's my turn at bat."

Behind him, the marine ground maintenance unit was hustling like mad to refuel and rearm the Blackhawk for immediate takeoff. While they loaded canisters of linked 20 mm cannon rounds for the minigun and fresh clusters of rockets for the underbelly launchers, the combat flight crew stood around, watching the work intently, making sure everything was done just right.

Bolan reached down and squeezed his old friend's uninjured hand. "Don't worry, Hal," he said. "If Samosa's taken the DIV, we'll get it back."

Brognola laughed at that. "Yeah, don't worry," he mocked.

"Just think about what those Mexican military sawbones are going to do your foot."

"They aren't going to do anything," Brognola said adamantly. "No painkillers. No stitches. Nothing. Just package me up for the flight to Bethesda and send me on my way."

"Señor," the lieutenant said to Bolan's back, "we're fueled and cleared to go."

The Executioner winked at Brognola, then turned to follow the young marine officer.

As they climbed back into the Blackhawk, the lieutenant said to him, "Your friend, there, he killed many cartel animals by himself, even though his leg is so bad he can hardly walk, and his hand looks like it's been run over by a truck. He is some kind of fighter. Kick-ass, I think you say." Admiration, touched with a little awe, was written all over the guy's face.

"Major kick-ass," Bolan agreed.

On the other side of the electrically fired minigun, a marine corporal sat already belted into a jump seat. The belly gunner who'd so thoroughly pounded the opposition on the hacienda road looked to be about nineteen years old. Though Bolan would never have wasted ammunition in that way, himself, he could understand the unit's need for payback, and the need to make some kind of indelible statement to an enemy that refused to die, that rose from its own ashes, again and again, animated by money, power and greed.

He liked these young men. He liked them instinctively. They were serious about their work. Professionals. Not as seasoned as he was, of course, but professionals just the same. The mission at hand, locating the missing drug-interdiction vessel, didn't call for any particular sort of subtlety, strategy or execution. It was either full-out search and rescue, or full-out search and destroy, at Bolan's discretion. Up to that moment, he had no confirmation that the ship had in fact been taken by the cartel, as both Brognola and he feared. Before calling in the massive air and sea support that might be necessary to subdue the high-tech warship, he had to find the DIV and evaluate the situation.

The pilot lifted the Blackhawk off the asphalt and flew due west, in the direction of the Pacific. In a few minutes, they passed over the offshore islands at two thousand feet, and climbing. The higher the Blackhawk flew, the more they could see.

Up to a point.

A mile above the water, out the open door of the cargo bay, Bolan could dimly make out both shorelines along the Sea of Cortez. The visibility was limited by the yellow-tinged haze coming off the mainland. The industrial smog had spread over the entire gulf. Bolan started scanning with binoculars as the pilot began a high-altitude grid search.

Of course, there was no guarantee that the *Bernardo Chinle* had sailed in the general direction they were traveling. It could have gone due south instead of west. And the DIV had the ability to hide in daylight, in plain sight, because it hadn't been officially reported as missing, yet. The commercial jet crews that overflew it wouldn't make any special note of its presence. And if it was far enough away from the normal shipping lanes, and it was a safe guess that it was, passing tankers and shrimpers wouldn't even see it.

Nobody but Bolan and the marines in the Blackhawk were looking for the *Bernardo Chinle*. Dropping off the radar wasn't grounds for an all-out search. It could have been part of the sea trials, though it hadn't been a scheduled exercise. The Blackhawk crew was proceeding on a suspicion that the vessel was in trouble, based in part on Brognola's information and the fact that it had broken all normal radio contact.

Eight minutes into the grid-pattern search, the pilot

sharply banked and turned southwest. A second later the lieutenant's voice came through Bolan's headset. Despite an effort to remain detached and unemotional, he was very excited. "Sir," he said, "we have just picked up an EPIRB signal from the *Bernardo Chinle*. We have the time of beacon's launch and its present coordinates."

"Is the ship in trouble?" Bolan asked. "Is it going down?"

"It's not that kind of beacon, sir," the lieutenant explained. "It operates on a different frequency than the usual emergency transmitter. It's the beacon the navy uses to mark drug shipments that have been thrown overboard. So they can find them after they run down the smugglers."

"They're not chasing drug runners," Bolan said.

"No, sir. Not this day."

"Pass on the position of the radio marker to your base commander," Bolan told him. Then he asked, "What's our ETA over the beacon?"

"Five minutes," the lieutenant replied. "Maybe a little less."

Three minutes later, the copilot leaned between the forward seats. He waved and pointed out his side window.

Bolan had already found the ship in the binoculars. From the thin ribbon of white water trailing off its stern, its engines were running. It was holding its position at idling speed. He could make out a second, smaller boat tied alongside the DIV's aft quarter, which seemed to support the theft hypothesis. The sport fishing boat might well have been the way the cartel pirates got on board. It was definitely the way they would get off, if they were going to scuttle the ship.

It was time to reduce the number of *ifs* in the equation.

"Take us down," the Executioner said into his headset microphone. "We need a closer look."

The pilot circled around 180 degrees, making his approach from the east, downwind and down current. He swept over the vessel's stern at a height of two hundred feet.

Bolan saw the Sikorsky helicopter parked on the rear flight deck. It looked like the same one he'd seen flying away from the hacienda earlier in the day. Which meant not only that Don Jorge Samosa might be on board to supervise the vessel's sinking, but there was a possibly that he'd brought his two sons as well.

That prospect didn't please Bolan.

Given the presence of the Hatteras alongside, it was likely that a number of cartel gunmen had boarded the ship. It was going to take guns and bullets, and spilled blood, to drive them off. The decks of the *Bernardo Chinle* would be turned into meat grinders. In that kind of situation, there was no way to guarantee the boys' safety.

A quarter mile off the DIV's port beam, the pilot swung the Blackhawk around again. No sooner had he turned, than he let out a curse. "Their radar is up!" he said.

"Jesus and Maria, we've been targeted!" the copilot cried. "They're going to launch rockets!"

"You can't run from them," Bolan said into his mike. "We've got to ditch. We've got to ditch, now!"

The marine pilot wasn't listening. His training had already kicked in. Training that told him he was empowered to abandon his aircraft only as a last resort. What he didn't realize was that the last resort was the only option he had left. He was already wheeling around in a steep bank, attempting to evade the unavoidable.

In a very few seconds they were going to have a flock of HEAT warhead-tipped rockets flying straight up their asses.

As the pilot accelerated out of the turn, Bolan reached for the chest buckle of his safety harness.

"FIRE, DAMMIT!" Samosa yelled at the seaman sitting at the control console beside Trevor Eames. "Didn't you hear what I said? What are you waiting for?"

The sailor heard, all right, but he didn't raise his hand to the on-screen keypad. He had obeyed the orders of the narco-terrorists up to that point. He had powered up the radar and fire control systems, acquired and locked in the airborne target and enabled a trio of rockets. But he hesitated over the last command.

The order to murder some of his own.

To murder those who had risked their lives to come to his and his shipmates' aid. In desperation, the sailor looked over at the admiral.

Eames could read the expression on his face. The man was silently begging, pleading for a direct order from his commanding officer, for permission either to comply or not to comply.

Admiral Fuentes, battered and bloodied, shook his head, no.

Eames slid his chair down the track in the floor until he could read the display screen over the uncooperative sailor's shoulder.

"The helicopter knows it's been locked in," he told the drug lord. "If we don't take it out immediately, it will confirm our position to its base and launch its own rockets at us."

"Somebody do something!" Samosa said. "Get that bastard out of the chair."

As Eames started to lunge for the sailor, the drug lord snatched a submachine gun from the hands of one of the Panamanian SEALs. His upper lip curled back in a snarl of fury, Don Jorge Samosa leaned over the top of the command console, aimed the commandeered weapon down at the seated man and opened fire, full-auto.

The hail of close-range 9 mm slugs momentarily pinned

the sailor against the seat back, torso, arms and legs juddering, then the chair swiveled slowly to the right, spilling him out onto the deck.

Eames jumped up and tapped the blood-splattered, on-screen keypad. At once, yellow flames and white smoke belched from the ASROC housing on the DIV's foredeck.

Rockets away.

Turning, Eames saw Admiral Fuentes staring at him fixedly, staring at him like he wanted to tear his arms out of their sockets and beat him to death with them. Fuentes knew who the traitor was.

But at this point what good would that knowledge do him?

Dead men can't hurt me, Eames told himself.

"THEY'VE LAUNCHED!" the Blackhawk's copilot shouted.

Those were the last words Bolan heard as he ripped off his communications headset. Already free of his safety harness, he lurched from the jump seat and across the deck of the cargo bay. Scooping up and slinging his weapons pack over his shoulder, the Executioner jumped out the open bay door.

He didn't say anything to the Mexican marines.

There wasn't time for goodbyes.

The fall to the water was only twenty-five feet. A cakewalk. It wasn't the fall that messed him up. It was the airspeed. It slammed him the instant he leapt from the cargo bay. When he hit the sea, his forward momentum cartwheeled him across the surface. The stunning, initial impact ripped the weapons pack right off his shoulder.

Overhead, things were going worse for the helicopter crew.

As he bounced and skipped over the water, the incoming rockets nailed the Blackhawk dead center. The air quaked from the tremendous explosion, which separated the main rotor from the fuselage, and sent a heap of burning wreckage tumbling into the sea not fifty feet ahead of him. As Bolan splashed to a stop, small pieces of debris pelted the surface all around him.

A ragged, metal rain.

The Executioner tread water, choking on the black smoke that boiled out of the twisted wreck.

The Blackhawk's fuselage only floated for a minute or two before filling with water and sliding beneath the surface.

As it went down, Bolan saw the marine pilot still strapped to his seat inside, charred to the bone, his uniform indistinguishable from flesh. The other crewmen were nowhere in sight. Their bodies had been vaporized by the direct hits from high explosive warheads.

At least death had been quick.

Bolan shook his head to clear the ringing from his ears.

With the marine helicopter knocked out of the air and sunk, apparently with all hands lost, the drug soldiers who'd seized the DIV wouldn't be expecting him.

That was the good news.

The bad news was that except for his SOG Pentagon knife, he was unarmed, and he had a quarter of a mile to swim before reaching the *Bernardo Chinle*. If he didn't make it to the ship before it was sent to the bottom, the swim got much, much longer.

Admiral Fuentes sagged back against the bridge's couch as the rockets whistled like banshees from their launch pod on his foredeck. He hurt inside, and his wounds were deeper than those merely of the flesh. Fuentes had never felt so helpless in his entire life. A man of action, of decision, through his entire professional life, he wasn't accustomed to helplessness. Even in the occasional, outnumbered, bar room brawls that had been part of his Annapolis days, he'd always had room to maneuver.

Because of the traitor, Eames, all avenues of retreat had been blocked. Escape for him and his crew seemed impossible.

Admiral Fuentes didn't watch the rockets blow the Blackhawk out of its low trajectory over the sea. He knew that it had happened from the cheers of the narco-terrorists on his bridge.

Fuentes was looking at the dead sailor on the deck. Remembering how the man had looked to him for guidance, for orders, and that the orders he'd given had cost the sailor his life.

For nothing, as it turned out.

What was I thinking? Fuentes asked himself. What other outcome was there?

He shut his eyes. The command to stand down had been an act of easy defiance for him. His own neck hadn't been in the noose. His regret was a sharp burning pain under his breastbone. Of course, he'd had no real choice in the matter. He couldn't order the murder of innocent people, not even to save his own crew.

When he opened his eyes, he stared at the man who had done the actual killing. Fuentes had heard one of the terrorists refer to him as "Don Jorge." Which under the circumstances, probably meant that he was none other than Don Jorge Luis Samosa, the Lord of the Seas. A fugitive from justice that Fuentes had long sought, but never seen.

Few if any law enforcement personnel had ever looked into the man's face, and of those who'd seen it, none had survived. Samosa was one of the most powerful criminals on the planet, and no one even knew what he looked like. That he had allowed the admiral to view him, up close, didn't bode well for his chances, or for the chances of his crew.

Fuentes turned his gaze on the two children who stood very close together in a corner of the bridge. It was clear from their conversation who they were. Apparently, Samosa had brought his sons along to witness the sinking of the *Bernardo Chinle*. He had also made them witness the slaughter of an unarmed man by his own hand.

If the drug lord was trying to demonstrate something to his sons, he had failed miserably.

Neither boy had been able to watch.

The younger one had clamped his hands over his ears and shut his eyes. The older boy had merely looked away, a blank expression on his face. A shell-shocked expression.

The princes of Hell were horrified by their inheritance.

Samosa didn't seem to notice. He was like a symphony conductor lost in the music that surrounded him. The destruction of the Marine helicopter pleased him immensely.

For Fuentes, hope was fast running out. Saving himself or any of his crew was looking more and more impossible.

If the Blackhawk crew hadn't managed to radio back to

base that they'd found the DIV and that they were under attack, or even if they had radioed, it was likely that the sinking of the ship would be over and done with before more rescuers arrived on the scene.

The Blackhawk had been his one-and-only chance.

As if to underscore that point, the drug lord announced, "It's time to clear the bridge of nonessential personnel."

When Fuentes looked up at him, he was smiling. "And that means you, Admiral."

Fuentes's big hands clenched into fists. Impotent fists.

At gunpoint, the narco-terrorists forced Fuentes and the bridge crew to their feet. As they were marched toward the door, the admiral suddenly turned and hawked a bloody gob right in the traitorous software designer's astonished face.

In response, one of the terrorists wound up and booted the admiral hard in the behind. Though the man grunted from the effort, Fuentes didn't even flinch. He leaned over the back of the control console. "I'll be waiting for you in hell," he assured Trevor Eames.

"Move, dammit!" the narco-terrorist said, cracking Fuentes across the back of the head with his SMG's forward grip. The impact on his skull made a hollow *thunk*.

The admiral saw stars, and would have fallen to the deck if the navigator hadn't caught him under an arm and held him up.

For Fuentes, getting down the bridge steps with a fractured knee was a difficult feat. He leaned heavily on the navigator's shoulder, trying to keep weight off the joint.

When they reached the main deck, their cartel captors headed them toward the stern with more kicks and smacks with their weapons, as if they were condemned men being marched en masse to the gallows. They walked with eyes downcast and their hearts riding high in their throats.

As he looked over the ship's rail, Fuentes realized that

this might well be the last time he ever saw the sky. Chances were good that he'd see the sea again, as it poured, uncontested, into his lungs.

Their two-man terrorist escort steered them off the main deck when they reached the secondary control tower, and made them descend the steep, metal stairway to the very bottom of the ship.

A short distance from the foot of the stairs, at the entrance to the DIV's main hold, another armed terrorist stood guard. Fuentes had little doubt as to why the guard was standing there, or what lay on the other side of the door.

A tomb.

When one of their escorts gave a signal, the guard unlocked the hold and pushed in the door. Then, using their gun butts, the three terrorists roughly shoved Fuentes and his bridge crew over the threshold.

The cargo area was large, but it looked bigger because it was so empty. The *Bernardo Chinle* wasn't carrying much in the way of supplies for its week of sea trials.

The crewmen already imprisoned there rose quickly to their feet from seats on boxes or on the deck. When the heavy door closed and locked behind them, some of the sailors let their weapons show. They had armed themselves with heavy wrenches and crowbars they'd found in the hold.

A pair of seamen rushed over and helped the navigator move the admiral to a seat on a wooden crate in the middle of the hold. He sat heavily, glad for the chance to rest his badly swollen knee.

As he took in the faces of his crew, Fuentes saw the fear in their eyes. He could smell it in the smotheringly hot air. There was a sense of betrayal as well, and it cut him to the core. Seeing the man they had entrusted with their lives, seeing how reduced, how bruised and bloodied, and at a loss for words he was, they knew they were doomed. It wouldn't be long before they panicked and started fighting one another.

Rats unable to flee the sinking ship.

What did they expect from him? A miracle? The ability to part walls of solid steel? Fuentes shifted position on the edge of the crate. Help wasn't going to arrive in time to save them. Of that, he was certain. He couldn't tell them that. Not when they were looking to him for hope, for leadership, for a goddamned plan.

He had to tell them something.

From experience, he knew his duty to his men was more complicated than just giving orders. Part of his responsibility as their commander was to give them comfort. Whether that comfort was realistic or not wasn't the issue, now or ever. The issue was, why should his crew die feeling helpless, feeling that there could have been something else they should have tried?

Pushing back the pain and fear, Admiral Fuentes said in the loud, clear voice of command, "Someone get me some duct tape."

For a minute the men just stared at him, dumbfounded. "On the double!"

One of the sailors broke ranks and rushed over to the tool cabinet along the wall. The doors were already standing open. He began rummaging inside at once.

When the roll of silver tape was delivered up to him, Fuentes thanked the seaman and took it. Then he held his injured leg out, stiffened from hip to ankle. Pulling free the tag end of the tape, he started wrapping it around the knee. He wrapped it tightly over his bloody trouser leg, binding it with many overlapping layers. He ripped the tape off at the roll. When he tested his leg, it was like a plank. There was no way he could bend it. Heaving himself up off the crate, he stood on it. He hopped around a little. It hurt but the pain was bearable, especially when he looked up and saw the expressions on the faces of his men.

"Now I'm ready to fight these bastards," he said. "Will you follow me?"

The sailors let loose an explosion of cheers.

The admiral let them vent their relief, then he gave them the only plan he had. "When the door opens again," he said, looking from man to man, "we will rush it, no matter what. If there are guns waiting for us, we will go over them. We drive the bastards into the deck with the weight of our bodies and when we have them down, we'll pound them to death and take their weapons. Understood?"

More whoops and war cries.

"Give me a crowbar," Fuentes said. When the length of forged steel was handed over to him, he hopped unassisted over to the door.

The message to his crew was clear: If there was gunfire, the admiral would take the very first bullets himself.

19

With no other options before him, and the certain knowledge that time was quickly running out, Mack Bolan put his face in the water and started swimming for the parked DIV.

Swimming distance was a mindlessly mechanical process, like jogging. Once in the flow of things, the strokes, the kicks and the breathing became automatic for him. He didn't have to think about them. It left him free to consider other things.

He thought about the crew of the Blackhawk. Fate had always been kind to the Executioner. He had dodged the bullet and beaten the odds countless times but he never took his decades-long streak of luck for granted. All he had to do was look behind him at the legions of the fallen to be humbled, to know that what had been given to him could and would one day be taken back.

He was saddened by the deaths of the marines, sorry that their glory had ended so soon. Too soon. As he swam toward the ship in the distance, plunging ahead one clean, efficient stroke after another, he sensed a warmth not from the sun, but from a radiance that filled him from the inside out.

The spirits of the dead lifted him.

Pure warrior spirits.

In his mind, the Executioner promised the hovering ghosts what they wanted, what they were waiting for.

Payback.

Fifty yards from the *Bernardo Chinle*'s hull, Bolan stopped swimming. He was on the side opposite from where the fishing boat was tied up. As he easily floated, his eyes and nose a few scant inches above water, he saw two men at the main deck's rail with submachine guns slung on shoulder straps. The one walking behind looked around furtively, then quickly threw a couple of empty green boxes over the side.

It was the wrong side of the ship, given the direction of the prevailing wind and sea.

When the boxes hit the water, they immediately drifted against the hull, and stayed there.

From this, and the fact that the box thrower and his companion were wearing shabby-looking, iridescent, two-piece business suits, Bolan concluded that they weren't sailors. From their dark complexions, they might have been Mexican, but they were in nobody's navy. More likely, they were soldiers in the army of Don Jorge Luis Samosa.

If the two gunmen had been looking Bolan's way, they could have seen his head sticking up out of the water. The guy who'd thrown the boxes leaned way over the rail, staring in dismay down at the floating containers, stunned that they hadn't sunk or drifted away. Realizing that that wasn't going to happen anytime soon, that he'd made a mistake, the soldier called his friend back to show him.

The other guy raised his hands to heaven in exasperation. Then he grabbed his partner by the lapels and gave him a hard shake.

Someone shouted at them from atop the signal bridge and the men stopped. Then the two of them ran up the stairs as fast as they could.

The Executioner ducked underwater and swam until all he could see in front of him was the gray side of the ship.

Then he surfaced, brushing the palm of his hand against the hull to make sure he stayed close to it and out of sight of the deck above. When his head popped out of the water, the discarded boxes were floating on either side of him. They were made of heavily waxed, green cardboard, which was why they hadn't gotten waterlogged.

The lettering on the sides read, C-4, Plastic Explosive.

As the boxes were both empty, Bolan had to assume that the explosive had already been placed in the DIV. Because cartel crew were still on board, the chances of immediate detonation and of sinking the *Bernardo Chinle* were slim.

Which meant the numbers hadn't started to fall for real, yet, and he had time to operate.

Bolan dog-paddled tight to the DIV's waterline, to the corner of the stern, and poked his head around it. To get to the chase boat's launch chute, he had to swim through fifty feet of prop wash. It was a daunting prospect, given the horsepower driving the huge blades directly beneath him. He had no choice but to go for it.

It was like swimming across a raging river, full of currents, whirlpools and eddies. By sticking close to the stern of the ship, he avoided the worst of it.

When he reached the mouth of the launch ramp, he found the end of a length of two-inch, nylon rope trailing from the top of the chute. After testing the rope to make sure it was well tied at the other end, he used it to pull himself up and in. For a moment, he rested there, clinging to the edge of the ramp's central groove. Then he climbed his way hand over hand to the top of the chute.

When he climbed, dripping wet, onto the platform beside it, he saw the discarded scuba tanks. And it was obvious to him how the assault team had gotten on board. There were eight of them.

Because he didn't know how many cartel soldiers had

boarded from the fishing boat or from Samosa's helicopter, he still had no idea how many guns he faced. His best guess, given the size of the Hatteras and the Sikorsky, was eighteen or twenty.

According to the marine base commander, the *Bernardo Chinle* had left port with a sea-trial crew of twenty-four sailors. Men who could either be a help or a hindrance to Bolan, depending on their physical condition. It was also possible that they were already dead, executed by the Samosa gangsters.

There were no firearms, no weapons of any kind left behind on the platform.

Moving to the bulkhead door on the back wall, Bolan drew the SOG Pentagon knife from its ankle sheath. The five-inch blade was razor-beveled on one side and serrated on the other. It was all he had to fight with.

For the time being.

He opened the bulkhead door and looked out onto a narrow hallway that intersected with a wider corridor after a short distance. There was no cover anywhere. Just gray metal walls, studded with rivets. Bolan advanced quickly to the next door on his right. He translated the words painted on it: Engine Room.

The bar-shaped handle yielded with a metallic clack. When he pushed the door inward, the ambient noise level took a giant leap. From a foot or two inside the doorway, he could see the new side-by-side engine blocks, each the size of an entire SUV. The huge diesels idled in a spotless compartment painted a brilliant high-gloss white. Along the far wall, in a separate console, were three computer screens. The screens were lighted up. There wasn't a soul around.

To Bolan, it looked like the Samosa forces had already swept the ship to round up its sailors. After capturing them, the next move would be to confine them in a single, secure location so they couldn't interfere with the sinking of the ship.

Bolan closed the door and continued down the hall, moving quickly. At the end of the corridor was a metal stairway. As he was on the bottom level of the ship, he had no place to go but up.

When he reached the second landing, which accessed the next deck, he heard a door slam shut. He backed against the bulkhead wall and stole a peek through the window in the landing's watertight door.

Down the gray hallway, he glimpsed a stocky Mexican in a business suit moving to the other side of the corridor. The Mexican had his back to the stairway, and Bolan. He carried a submachine gun with a collapsible-rear stock on a shoulder sling.

The drug soldier hurriedly entered a room, leaving the door open behind him.

The Executioner had his hand on the door latch, already pressing down, about to make his move, when the guy suddenly reappeared in the hallway. He closed the door securely behind him, then rushed back to the other side of the hall, coat flapping, and entered the next room in line. As before, he left the door behind him open.

Whatever the cartel thug was doing, he was doing it as fast as he possibly could.

Bolan cracked open the stairway door and slipped through it. With the Pentagon in his right hand, he ran in long, loping strides, closing the distance between himself and the open doorway.

His mind was perfectly clear as he jumped into the room. He was anticipating nothing and everything, ready to react with savage force to whatever he found.

As it turned out, the hapless drug soldier still had his back to Bolan. His arms were stretched high above his head. His Heckler & Koch MP-5 was dangling uselessly over his shoulder on its sling. The Mexican was caught flat-footed, in the process of sealing the porthole.

The drug soldier grunted in surprise at the sudden intrusion, head automatically twisting over his shoulder, eyes widening as he saw the big man coming at him with the blade in his hand.

Before the Mexican could fully turn, before he could get out another sound, Bolan had spanned the gap between them. He used his momentum to slam the gunner's head and shoulders up against the bunk frame. Then he plunged the point of the Pentagon under the man's chin, driving the blade upward, through the bottom of his tongue, skewering it, then through the top of his throat and into the thin shelf of bone that protected the base of his brain.

The impaled drug soldier made a terrible, choking noise, his arms flapped rigidly at his sides, the tendons in his neck standing out like steel cables, and his eyes squeezed tightly shut in pain and shock.

Bolan whacked the knife's pommel hard with the heel of his hand, driving the blade in another half inch.

The critical half inch.

In a rush, all the life went out of the soldier. He stopped struggling and slipped limply to the deck.

Bolan turned him over onto his back. He had to use considerable brute force to wedge and pry the blade free of the grip of the man's skull. And when the knife came free, it released a torrent of backed-up blood from severed vessels temporarily sealed by the blade's sideways pressure.

The Executioner stepped aside to avoid being splashed, then rolled the man onto his face. With a quick slash of the SOG's serrated edge, he cut through the Heckler & Koch's web strap, freeing the weapon from the back of its dead owner. As the strap was dripping blood, he cut it off at the buckles. Then he wiped both sides of the blade on the soldier's pants.

Checking the chamber for a live round and finding none, he dumped the magazine into his palm. The round count was full. Snapping the magazine back into the gun, he gave the charging handle a flick, chambering the first full-metal jacket. It surprised him a little that the drug soldier was carrying a weapon that wasn't ready to fire. The soldier had been confident that whatever opposition there was had already been taken care of.

Bolan paused at the room's doorway, listening hard. In the distance he heard more hatches and doors being slammed. Somebody was going to a lot of trouble to make sure the contents of the DIV stayed inside once its hull was breached.

The Lord of the Seas wanted no incriminating evidence floating to the surface.

It also explained why the other hardman had been so upset to see the empty C-4 containers bobbing in the water, and why the two of them had scampered off so quickly, before anyone of a higher rank could get a look at what they'd done.

Bolan followed the sounds down the hall to an interior staircase amidships. Looking down over the railing, he saw movement on the deck below. A man with black hair was standing with his back to a closed watertight door. He was carrying the same kind of gun Bolan had taken from the dead guy. From the weapon and his position in the hallway, it was plain that he was keeping watch on something or someone secured on the other side of the door.

Moving as quietly as he could, the Executioner descended the steps. Though he now had a functioning firearm, he was hesitant to use it because of the noise and probability it would draw unwanted attention his way. He shifted the MP-5 to his left hand and drew out the Pentagon with his right.

The weapon had no cross guard. But for the double-edge configuration and the Kraton handle, tacky to the touch, it was shaped like a throwing knife. Bolan gripped the blade by the point as he came down the last flight of steps.

The guard was to his right, hidden from view by the steps and the railing. Bolan stopped three stairs from the bottom, leaned out over the rail and cocked his right arm back.

The drug soldier didn't notice him until it was too late, until the Pentagon was spinning through the air. As he looked up, raising his chin from his chest, the blade sank into his throat all the way to the hilt.

Gagging, his eyes bugging, the man grabbed the handle with both hands and tried to pull it free.

He couldn't.

Bolan vaulted the stair rail and charged him, full-tilt.

The soldier gave up on the knife, released the handle and tried to get his SMG and swing it up on its shoulder strap.

There wasn't enough time.

As the muzzle came up, the Executioner banged the barrel aside with his own. Then he reached across his chest and grabbed the knife handle. With a single yank, he ripped it from the man's throat and in the process opened a six-inch gash along the side of his neck. Blood from the slashed arteries spurted across the corridor.

Not a sound escaped the man's parted, astonished lips. He sank to his knees on the deck, watching in absolute terror as his life ebbed away in pulsing jets of crimson.

It didn't take long for that to happen, no more than a few seconds, and by then the soldier was flat on his face, deathly pale and dead still. His heart had pumped itself dry.

Bolan put his ear to the watertight door of the hold. He could hear men talking in low voices on the other side. At least he knew where the crew of the *Bernardo Chinle*'s was and that they were still alive.

Taking a step back and shifting the automatic weapon to his strong hand, he called out in Spanish in a loud, clear voice, "Stand away from the door. I'm going to open it."

With that, he reached for the door handle and lifted it up.

20

Even though he was standing right beside the door, Admiral Fuentes didn't hear the one-sided, life-and-death struggle in the hallway a few feet away. None of the other sailors heard it, either. But there was no mistaking the man's voice booming against the other side of the door, warning them that he was about to open it.

Grinning, the sailors bunched behind their commander, ready to follow him into Hell, if necessary. It was the miracle they had all prayed for, a last chance to fight and maybe survive.

The door handle lifted, then the door swung inward.

Fuentes wasn't thinking about his dying in the next few seconds. He wasn't thinking about the pain of close-range bullets breaking his bones, shredding his vital organs. He wasn't thinking about anything but moving forward, of throwing himself at whoever had opened the door.

When the admiral hopped over the threshold with the crowbar raised high over his head, he immediately slipped in all the blood that lay puddled on the deck. Fuentes caught himself only by reaching back and grabbing the arm of one of the sailors behind him. A glance down told him that the blood had come from the facedown cartel soldier, the same guy who had been guarding the door to the hold.

The man who'd apparently opened the door for them

had already retreated down the corridor to the stairwell twenty feet away, and was well out of reach.

Fuentes had never seen the blue-eyed gringo before. He was tall, lean and muscular. And he was soaking wet. Not from blood; from water, seawater most likely. He carried the Heckler & Koch easily. It was leveled at the admiral's chest. Another MP-5, probably taken from the dead guard, lay on the deck at his feet.

As the rest of the crew of the *Bernardo Chinle* rushed out into the hallway and surrounded Fuentes, the gringo said evenly, "Everybody just stay right where they are."

"What do you think you're going to do with that gun?" Fuentes fumed at him. He waved the crowbar over his head, threateningly. "Do you think you're going to be able to shoot us all before we get to you?"

The gringo looked over the gang of seamen, then at the curved magazine of the MP-5 A3. "I've got thirty rounds in here," he said, flatly. "That means I can shoot some of you twice."

Something in the man's face told Fuentes he wasn't just bragging in order to back them down. The admiral looked at the dead man at his feet, and the anger and fear that had pushed him to the point of desperation and virtual suicide seemed to lose its edge. "What happened to this guy?" he said. "Did you kill him?"

"He didn't want to let you boys out," the gringo said, "so I had to convince him."

"If you're not a drug soldier," Fuentes said, "then who in the hell are you? You're obviously an American. Are you DEA? CIA? How did you get on board?"

The gringo shook his head. He wasn't going to answer any more questions. "Maybe our time would be better spent figuring out how to retake this ship," he said.

Fuentes lowered the crowbar. The stranger had a point. Whoever he was, he was clearly on the side of the crew, or he wouldn't have risked his own life to cut the throat of the drug soldier guarding them.

"You're right," Fuentes said. "I apologize. Please excuse our apparent lack of gratitude. We thought we were about to die."

"You're not out of the woods, yet, I'm afraid."

"Right again," Fuentes said. "The cartel crew has already placed explosives in the bilges. We don't have much time if we're going to save the ship and ourselves."

"We can't regain control of the bridge with sheer numbers," the gringo told him. He bent and picked up the submachine gun from the deck, then he handed it butt-first to Fuentes. "We're going to need more guns than these."

"There are weapons locked in the armory," the admiral said. He waved to his men. "Let's go. Quick!"

The small arms locker on the *Bernardo Chinle* was located on the port side, on the ground level. Because Fuentes and the tall gringo were the only men armed, they took the lead.

They came across no cartel thugs between the hold and the door of the weapons locker. Evidently they had moved to a different part of the ship.

The armory door was protected by a heavy padlock, which one of the sailors unlocked. Inside the small low-ceilinged room in steel racks on the metal walls were a double row of G-3 assault rifles in 7.62 mm NATO. The 20-round box magazines, preloaded, sat in bins along the foot of the wall. In another locked cabinet, Colt .45 M-1911 autopistols were displayed, butts first. The seaman started hurriedly passing out the weapons and bullets.

Fuentes hobbled through the room past them. As he did, he waved for the tall gringo to follow him. At the far wall, he bent over a wooden crate on the floor and flipped up the lid.

"Do you know how to use one of those?" he said, pointing at the length of shock-mounted, plastic pipe.

On the side of the olive drab crate, stenciled in black, were the letters: M-72 A2 LAW.

"Yeah, I do," the gringo said.

"Well, that makes two of us," Fuentes told him. He handed the American one of the 66 mm rocket launchers, then said, "If the narco-terrorists have the main bridge battened down, we won't be able to break in. With these HEAT warheads we can blast the doors right off their hinges."

Slipping the LAW's built-in sling over his shoulder, the admiral picked out a second launcher tube for himself, then returned to the front of the room to address his men.

"It's necessary," he said, "that we divide our force in two. There's not enough room for all of us to charge the bridge along one side of the ship. If we try, we'll get tangled up with one another and bottled along the rail. We'll be too easy for the enemy to kill. If we split up, we can come at them from two directions at once, along the starboard rail and over the top to the bridge roof."

Fuentes looked over at the gringo. "I will take our new friend, here," he said, "and the men on this side of the room. We will travel the low road, over the main deck." Then he pointed at the ship's navigator and said, "You take the others and lead them over the top."

The navigator nodded.

"If you make contact with the terrorists," Fuentes went on, "press them with everything you've got. Push them into the sea if you can. We've got numbers equal to theirs and we know the ship better. We can win this. I'm sure of it."

As the sailors filed out of the armory, the blue-eyed gringo traded his MP-5 for one of the Heckler & Koch G-3s and a handful of loaded magazines. The reason was obvious. The assault rifle's cartridge packed considerably more wallop than the 9 mm Parabellum.

As the admiral walked stiff-legged toward the door, the American looked down at the wadded band of duct tape that held his knee rigid and said, "You could stay here, you know. That leg is only going to get in the way. It might get you killed."

"This is my ship," Fuentes said. "My command. I won't sit out this battle."

In truth, his leg hurt like hell. When it wasn't both throbbing and aching, it felt like someone was reaming it out with a three-eighths-inch power drill. And to immobilize it, he'd wrapped himself up so tightly that he'd cut off most of the circulation to his foot.

It was a short distance to the bridge, he told himself. To save his ship and his crew, he could walk on his hands that far.

In the hallway outside the armory, the two groups split up. The high-road platoon headed for the stairway that led up to the second level, which connected across the signal deck to the bridge's roof. Fuentes and the American took their ten men and headed down the corridor for the door to the main deck, starboard side.

The admiral noticed how comfortable the gringo seemed with an assault rifle in his hand. Though he hadn't touched that particular weapon before, it was already like a part of him, an extension of his arm and brain. In his military career, Fuentes had met a few other men who knew their weapons that well. Professional soldiers. Mercenaries. Men of precision and control, not like the cartel's drug soldiers, who were little more than glorified street thugs. Men to be a little afraid of, always. Even when they slept.

As they paused at the door to the main deck, the gringo turned to him and said, "Did you actually see Don Jorge

Samosa? Can you confirm that he's on board? Did he have his children with him?''

"I don't know if it was Samosa or not," Fuentes replied. "He didn't bother giving me his name, but he did have two young boys with him. Both of them were under ten. They were on the bridge when my crew was led down to the hold."

A shadow passed over the tall man's face.

An ice-cold shadow.

"The bastard shot one of my crew right in front of them," Fuentes continued, fighting down a sudden uneasy feeling about the man who stood so close to him. "He didn't tell the two boys to turn away or anything when he did it. It was as if he wanted them to see the murder. And you say they were his children? Some father!"

Without a word of explanation, the gringo turned away and headed down the line of armed men waiting in the corridor behind him. He spoke quickly to each crewman in turn, and he stepped in almost nose to nose to do it.

Fuentes only heard what he said to the first sailor, but it became apparent that he was saying the same thing to each man in turn.

What he said was this: "There are two young boys on the bridge of this ship. They are innocent victims here. If you shoot them, even by accident, I will kill you without hesitation."

When the gringo returned to the admiral and the front of the line, he said, "You overheard what I told your men?"

Fuentes nodded.

"Good, then I don't have to repeat it to you."

The admiral just stared at him for a second. The look in the tall man's eyes said he had drawn a line in the sand. A straight line. It said, disregard my warning at your own peril.

This gringo made up his own rules.

And then he enforced them.

Fuentes was glad the man was on his side.

Then the gringo moved close to him again, making the uneasy feelings in his stomach resurface. In a low voice that only Fuentes could hear, he said, "I know you want to lead your men, Admiral, but it might be better if you let the others go first. You can't move quickly enough on that leg to take the point. We can't afford to get bogged down between here and the bridge. If we do, many of your sailors will die needlessly."

Fuentes was momentarily taken aback. Of course, the American's assessment was right on target. The admiral was only thinking about his own revenge, about getting his ship back, not about the danger his hobbled leg presented to others under his command.

The admiral stepped to the side, out of the way.

The gringo went through the door first. Fuentes waved for his men to follow. Then he brought up the rear, limping badly.

21

Ignacio Nuñez regarded the two Mexican gunmen standing before him with a mixture of contempt and fury. He didn't know either of their names. He didn't want to know. When he needed their full attention, he shouted at them.

"Hey!" he yelled.

They blinked at him.

Looking into the flat roundness of their eyes, he was reminded of the dumb beasts of the field. These were dull, stubborn, stupid and sullen men.

In their faces he could read their opinion of him, as well. It turned out the affection between the three of them was mutual. They thought he was a high-strung asshole, puffed up with self-importance, and much, much less manly than they were.

He pointed at the pair of empty boxes of C-4 that one of the men carried. The Mexican wanted to dump them over the side because it was easier, and because he was too damned lazy to do the job right. "The cardboard won't sink," he told the man for the third time. "You can't just throw those overboard. Take the boxes with you below-decks and seal them in a room."

The Mexican half smiled at him in a most infuriating way. It was like saying, "You're not really my boss. You're just a Panamanian. You don't know anything."

Babysitting a couple of morons was service above and beyond as far as Nuñez was concerned, but under the circumstances, there was nothing he could do about it. He was convinced that unless he kept close tabs on them, they would do something stupid, either by accident or on purpose, like leaving a hatch open just to show him what they thought of his orders, and to let him know who's the boss.

Under other combat or mission conditions, Nuñez would have shot them both, with pleasure and without warning. He had the distinct feeling that they would have done the same.

"Finish up in the crew quarters," he told the Mexicans. "I'm going forward to batten down the galley." He paused to check his wristwatch, then added, "Meet me by the stack on the first level in five minutes. Is that understood?"

The Mexicans shrugged noncommittally.

Nuñez scowled at them. Before he could repeat the order, they turned for the stern and started walking slowly, insolently away.

Maybe, just maybe, they wouldn't screw up the job. After all, it only required them to clear the corridors of any loose debris and shut the cabin windows and doors. "Idiots!" the SEAL spit at their wide backs. Then he broke into a jog, heading for the stairs.

After sealing the ship's kitchen area, Nuñez returned to the middle deck. Salvator and Raimundo and their Mexicans were waiting for him beside the stack. His own Mexicans were nowhere in sight.

"Everything shut up nice and tight?" Nuñez said to his SEALs.

"All secure to midships," Salvator said.

Raimundo gave him a thumbs-up.

He looked toward the stern, grinding his teeth. Where were those other assholes?

Just when he thought they were going to make him go look for them as some kind of ridiculous payback, the two

Mexicans appeared around a corner of the superstructure. They were actually running.

When they joined the group, red-faced and out of breath, the SEAL leader took out his blueprint of the DIV's decks and began making the assignments to shut up the forward part of the ship. As he divided the coverage, his attention kept wandering back to his two Mexicans. They seemed very pleased with themselves, like they were sharing a private joke. At his expense. It was most irritating.

When the assignments were given out, Nuñez said, "Break time is over. Let's finish the job."

Nuñez started climbing the flight steps that led to the bridge roof. The Mexicans trudged behind him. Salvator and Raimundo were in the process of moving their men to the port and starboard stairways, respectively. All nine of them were still on the signal deck when a hail of automatic weapon fire rained around them.

It was a hell-squall of whining, ricocheting bullets.

As Nuñez looked over his shoulder to locate the source of the gunfire, he saw the Mexican below him on the steps absorb hits from what had to be a half-dozen heavy-caliber rifle slugs. The bullets shook him like a rag toy, sending clumps of spongy red matter exploding from the front of his shirt and suit jacket, and splattering the steps in front of him. The Mexican looked up at the SEAL, an expression of agony and desperation on his face. The shock trauma had cost him his grip on the stairway railing. His legs were giving out under him. He was falling backward.

His blood-flecked lips formed the silent words, "Help me!"

Caught in the middle of the kill zone, Nuñez turned without offering a hand and, under concentrated autofire, leapt up the remaining steps to the cover of a ventilation pipe.

As he brought his weapon up, the other Mexican came

scrambling over the top of the stairs. Ridiculously, he was covering the back of his head with his hands, as if he was trying to outrun an unexpected rainstorm.

This rainstorm made dents in the deck on both sides of him, gouging bright spots through the radar-deflecting paint. And the raindrops didn't just spatter the backs of his upraised hands. They went through them.

The Mexican was slammed to the deck by a flurry of hits to his head and shoulders. And as he went down, the bullet strikes continued, making him flop and jerk.

The shooters had the high ground on them and they had to have ammo to spare because they put another dozen rounds into the dead Mexican, turning the back of his suit jacket into a gory mess.

Nuñez looked up around the vent pipe. He caught the muzzle-flashes coming from the top of the stack, just below the radio mast.

When the shooting finally stopped, Salvator yelled up from the signal deck. "Who the hell is it?"

"Got to be the sailors," Nuñez shouted down at him. "They've gotten free somehow, made it to the armory and picked up guns."

The real bitch was, they'd managed to sneak in behind Nuñez's crew and take positions in the tower. Which meant they controlled the deck between the stack and the bridge.

Even so, sailors were no match for SEALs.

Nuñez switched his submachine gun fire selector to single, then he stood and braced his weapon against the side of the pipe. Immediately, he put the sights on the spot where he'd seen one of the shooters. The guy was still there, his head and shoulders backlit as he looked down on the deck. The range was no more than eighty feet. A piece of cake. Nuñez punched out six quick single shots. He didn't pay attention to the falling bullets, the puffs of dust and sparks off the legs of the steel tower, because he knew it would only slow his pace. His goal was to put as many aimed shots into the area as possible in the shortest time.

On the fifth shot, the sailor-sniper dropped his rifle. On the sixth, he fell from the stack headfirst, arms spread wide. As Nuñez ducked back to cover, the other shooter up there poured automatic fire onto his position. Even with the bullets pounding against the vent pipe, he heard the falling sailor hit the deck. The body made a solid thud accompanied by the sharp crack of a breaking neck.

The SEAL leader did a quick mental tally of the total number of men his team could be facing. There were twenty-four crewmen on the ship to start with, and that counted the traitor, Eames. Minus him, minus the dead officer, the sonar man on the bridge and the sailor he'd just killed, that left twenty able bodies for them to deal with.

It was doable.

But first, they had to clear the stack of the other sniper. "Salvator, Raimundo!" Nuñez shouted. "Triangular!"

Under his breath, the SEAL leader counted to five slowly. It was a maneuver he and his men had practiced and used in similar situations before, with devastating results. On the count of five, Nuñez popped up again. Below, on either side of the signal deck, Salvator and Raimundo did the same. They didn't all open fire at exactly the same instant, but it was very close.

Nuñez pinned the trigger of his MP-5, streaming 9 mm fire up into the base of the radar mast where the second sniper had his hide. The other two SEALs did likewise. The three-pronged attack poured blistering gunfire onto the target, literally disintegrating the radar mast.

The sniper tried to pull back, but he had nowhere to run. Caught in the cross fire, he was hit a dozen times before all three SMGs came up empty. No longer held in place by the impact of the bullets, he slipped from his perch and cartwheeled four stories to the deck.

Nuñez moved from the vent pipe to the back rail of the signal deck. As he did, he stripped and discarded the spent magazine and quickly reloaded his weapon. Looking over the rail, he saw two groups of sailors burst through the doors at the first level. Moving rapidly, they fired on Salvator and Raimundo, beating them back toward the bow.

Now Nuñez had the high ground, and he used it to advantage. Shouldering the H&K, he laid down covering fire for his fellow SEALs and their Mexicans. With aimed single shots, he pinned the sailors along the sides of the smokestack, allowing Salvator and Raimundo to reach the base of the stairs leading to the signal deck.

He wasn't trying to kill the crewmen, that would've meant taking more time with each target, waiting until a man showed himself. He couldn't do that and maintain control of the field. His goal was to make the sailors keep their heads down until his men could mount the steps.

Salvator, Raimundo and the others were halfway up when the sailors realized what was about to happen. Instead of having one gun pointed down at them, they were about to have seven. Ignoring Nuñez's fire, they jumped out from behind their cover and opened up on the men on the stairway with everything they had.

Nuñez killed one of them, for sure. He could tell by the way the man's arms flew up, and the way he bounced when he hit the deck. By the time he'd acquired another running target, Salvator dashed up the top step. Raimundo was right on his heels.

Both men turned at once and started shooting at the sailors below.

The sounds of battle rolled over the ship.

The shooting was coming not only from the first level

directly below them, but from behind them, along the starboard side of the main deck. Nuñez realized at once that the ship's crew had divided in order to create two lines of attack, that more freed sailors were fighting their way toward the bridge. At that moment, there was absolutely nothing he could do about it.

Three of the Mexicans made it up the steps, and of those three, only two made it without getting hit. The wounded man took a round in his thigh. Clutching his leg in both hands, he speed-hopped past the SEALs, toward the stairs to the bridge roof. The other four cartel soldiers got trapped on the staircase and, despite the Panamanian's cover, were torn apart by tightly grouped autofire from a half-dozen weapons.

Perhaps emboldened by this victory, the sailors pressed forward, crossing the flat hellscape of the signal deck under the blazing guns of Nuñez and his SEALs.

The Panamanians killed three more crewmen in short order, blasting them apart as they tried to reach the corpse-choked foot of the stairway.

The remaining four sailors immediately started to pull back to the sides of the smokestack in order to regroup. As they did so, Nuñez took careful aim and, with a swinging lead on his target, fired one shot, hitting a man in the back of the head.

It had to be a glancing wound because the sailor didn't drop like a puppet with cut strings. Instead, he staggered away from the direction of cover in an apparent, half-conscious daze. Operating on autopilot, he was stumbling like a drunk, trying desperately to keep his balance and his legs under him.

From positions of safety, his comrades waved and yelled for him to get down.

Too late.

From the rail one story above, three submachine guns

belched flame in unison and the wall of lead they unleashed slammed the man face-first onto the deck.

When Nuñez, Salvator and Raimundo stopped firing, they could hear the continuing battle behind them, two levels down along the starboard rail.

The SEAL leader turned from the signal deck and ran toward the bridge's starboard wing. He was fifteen feet from the solid wall that protected the edge of the wing platform when there was a tremendous explosion from below and the deck beneath his feet shuddered and rippled.

He fell, hard, smacking his nose and chin on the deck. Pushing up from his stomach, he tasted the blood in his mouth.

The crew of the *Bernardo Chinle* had escalated the battle.

When he looked over the wing rail, he saw the effects of a 66 mm HEAT warhead. The lower staircase was a heap of twisted metal. The bodies of the two men lay tangled in it, their torsos ripped open, their guts plundered by the blast.

Then a tall, dark-haired man stepped into view on the main deck directly below him. A grin spread over Nuñez's face. Sighting his MP-5 over the railing, the Panamanian SEAL licked the blood off his teeth.

22

As Bolan stepped through the doorway and onto the DIV's main deck, gunfire broke out on the first level, forward of his position. The other group of sailors had already engaged the enemy. Bolan could only hear the thundering clatter of 7.62 mm NATO rounds. From the sounds of things, the crewmen had caught the cartel soldiers with their pants down.

The advantage was short-lived, however.

After a few seconds, the sailors' fire was answered. The Executioner recognized the canvas-ripping bark of 9 mm submachine guns. Lots of them.

Waving the men behind him onward, Bolan took off running up the starboard side of the ship. Whether the sailors on his team were concerned about all the shooting above them, or whether they were feeling uneasy about carrying side arms into a full-out firefight, they hung back from his point a bit more than he was comfortable with because it tended to string them out too much along the rail.

Realizing the danger they were putting themselves in, he shouted, "Come on! Hurry up! Close it up!"

The Executioner's back was momentarily turned to the bow when they took fire from the bottom of the staircase leading up to the bridge. Bullets whined furiously past him, sparking off the deck, singing off the rail.

Bolan sidestepped into a doorway. The door was shut

and when he tried the handle, he realized it was locked from the inside. But when he put his back flat to it, its slight recess, coupled with the curve of the wall forward, protected him from the flying lead.

Two of the sailors coming up behind him weren't so lucky. They both went down under the first withering volley. One was badly gut-shot. He curled up around the wound in his lower abdomen, kicking his legs, breakdancing in a wild circle on the deck. The other sailor's head exploded. From the eyes up, his skull and its contents simply vanished, only to reappear as a line of pink slime strewed along the deck behind him. The rate of hostile fire was such that his corpse was hit and twisted by another five or ten bullets before it toppled over the rail.

Bolan watched the soles of his bare feet disappear. The sailor's shoes remained on the deck, where he had been shot out of them. When the Executioner looked back toward the stern, he was relieved to see the other sailors had followed his lead and flattened themselves hard against the superstructure.

Bolan leaned his head past the door's recess to get a peek at the opposition. He ducked back immediately as more bullets screamed down the deck. The slugs skipped harmlessly off the wall in front of him, veering over the rail and into the sea.

There were two shooters in the bow, both of them crouching behind the staircase leading to the bridge, both firing with their muzzles poking out between the stairs' metal treads.

It presented an ugly scenario.

Bolan's group couldn't advance into the waiting guns without getting turned into hamburger. And if they tried to retreat, the result would be the same. Whatever element of surprise they had going for them was long gone.

Desperate times called for desperate measures.

Even overkill.

As Bolan unslung the LAW launcher from over his shoulder, something roared past him at chest height from his right.

Because he knew in an instant what it was, and what it would do, he reacted with pure instinct, throwing his forearm up to protect the right side of his face. Down the deck, sixty feet away, the stairway exploded in a rocking, earsplitting thunderclap.

The metal treads were turned into shrapnel by the blast of the HEAT warhead. One of the steps skittered to a stop a yard from Bolan's foot. It was scorched black and dented in the middle, as if a giant boot had stomped it.

When the Executioner stuck his head out again, he saw there was nothing left of the bottom six steps. Suspended from the wall above, the incomplete stairway hung above a heap of twisted, fire-blackened metal. Each of the bodies that lay behind it had been nearly torn in two. Their clothing smoldered and burned, putting up a greasy, dark smoke.

Bolan turned toward the stern. At the rear of the line of sailors, Admiral Fuentes stood in the middle of the deck. He still had the LAW launch tube on his shoulder. The naval officer had stepped out into the death zone, into full view of the shooters to discharge the HEAT-tipped rocket.

"Move!" he shouted to his men as he tossed the spent launcher over the side. To emphasize his point, he clapped his hands sharply.

The sailors immediately moved out from cover.

From the decks above, gunfire continued to rage back and forth. To Bolan, it sounded like the other group of sailors had gotten bogged down short of their goal. They hadn't been able to advance against the drug soldiers defending the back-door route to the bridge.

It had become a shooting gallery.

It was a recipe for complete disaster, if Bolan's unit didn't advance to the upper level quickly.

Bolan pushed ahead on a dead run to the foot of the ruined stairs. Glancing back, he saw Fuentes standing over the belly-wounded sailor, trying to help him.

On the bridge above and behind Bolan something moved. Something threatening.

As a spray of Parabellums spanged bright spots into the deck, the Executioner stepped under the overhang of the bridge wing out of the line of fire.

The sailors down the deck were running right into trouble. Leaning out, he waved them tighter to the superstructure.

One guy didn't move quite far enough. As the others stepped aside, he was hit by a single, downward-angled head shot from the upper rail. The impact of the bullet snapped his head hard to the right and, for an instant, his temple touched his shoulder.

He hit the deck like a bag of cement.

In another second or two, four soldiers had joined Bolan beside the wall. They looked scared, but determined.

"Wait until after I clear the way, then move up and take covering positions," he told them.

With that, he stepped away from the protection of the overhang with the G-3 assault rifle tight to his shoulder and its muzzle pointing almost straight up. He kept backing up, away from the wall, toward the staircase. The instant he could see the top edge of the bridge rail, he opened fire, full-auto. With a surgical sweep of the weapon's muzzle, he clipped the front of the rail with a string of heavy-caliber slugs. The autorifle's deafening clatter mixed with the dull clang of lead shattering on steel.

If the shooter was still up there waiting for a second chance at him, the volley of autofire drove him back and kept him back.

"Come on! Move!" Bolan shouted to the sailors, waving them out from the protection of the superstructure.

The crewmen did exactly as they had been told. They hustled behind the ruined steps and, aiming their weapons up, provided cover for the group's advance to the bridge.

The Executioner had to shoulder-sling his assault rifle in order to climb over the wrecked section of the steps and reach the undamaged portion. As he pulled himself up onto the seventh step, the sailors below him cut loose a blast of bullets.

He unslung the G-3 and moved up the rickety staircase to the bend of the landing. When he looked around the corner, the way ahead was clear for the moment. He didn't like the way the staircase swayed under his weight. He had doubts that it would hold more than two men at once.

Turning back, he yelled down to the sailors. "One at a time. Now!"

No sooner had he spoken than something creaked around the turn above him. Beneath his legs, the suspended staircase vibrated and shimmied from heavy footsteps.

Bolan shoved the barrel of the assault rifle around the corner. He fired blind, fanning the muzzle back and forth.

Amid the full-auto chatter, he heard a definite grunt, then the staircase really started to shake.

Ten sickening bumps before the corpse of a Mexican in a cheap suit slid down onto the landing in front of him.

"Hold it!" he called to the sailor starting to mount the stairs below.

He grabbed the cartel soldier by the ankles of his cowboy boots and hauled him off the landing, then he gave the man's warm body a shove down the steps. He had to brace himself as the corpse bumped and the staircase trembled. The body spilled off the seventh step and landed on its side on the deck below.

As the Executioner pressed on, starting around the bend,

shots from above forced him to pull back again. He caught sight of somebody standing at the top of the stairs on the bridge deck, blocking his path.

To take the bridge he had to get to the top of the stairs. There was no way around it.

He stuck the G-3 around the corner again. Touching off a short burst, he rounded the bend.

The way above was clear. He took the first two steps in a single bound.

Suddenly, a blocky form moved into position above him. The drug soldier swung the sights of an automatic weapon down on him.

Bolan opened fire first and the man took hits in the legs and groin. He staggered back, returning fire in a wild spray.

The Executioner flattened on the steps, his own weapon still clattering in his fist as the cartel thug's bullets screamed over his head.

The kill wasn't clean and it wasn't pretty.

A flurry of 7.62 mm NATO rounds opened the soldier from the belly to the forehead. Their jarring impact hurled him against the exterior wall of the bridge, bounced him off and sent him tumbling headfirst down the stairs.

Bolan rolled to his back, letting the body slide by him.

It came to a rest on the landing below.

The staircase was still shaking as Bolan stripped the G-3's nearly empty mag and replaced it. As he chambered the first round in the stack, another shooter appeared on the bridge deck directly above him. There was no time to turn. The Executioner fired from his back, upside down, drawing a line of bullets from the top step up the gunman's torso.

It dropped the Mexican to his knees.

In slow motion, he lowered his weapon, put the palms

of his hands on the bridge deck and looked down in astonishment at the man who was about to kill him.

His executioner.

Bolan rolled over and shot him once through the face. Then he called down to the crewmen waiting below, "Come on, move up!"

When he reached the top of the steps, peering over the shoulder of the Mexican corpse, he could see the wall of the bridge and its heavy door, both marked by bullet strikes.

Gunfire rattled at him. As he lowered his head, slugs thwacked into the butt and back of the dead Mexican. Bolan moved back down the stairs a little to avoid the splash.

He'd gotten a glimpse of the shooters. One was on the bridge roof, the other had a higher position behind the railing.

They had excellent shooting angles on him. Because they were stationed so far apart, he couldn't hope to pin both of them down with his own covering fire. In order to reach the safety of the bridge wall and door, he would have to get over the corpse, then cross ten feet of open space.

Two guns could keep him pinned there until hell froze over.

If he let them.

The staircase trembled as the sailor crawled to the landing below him. The man's fingers were red from the blood that had leaked out of the dead Mexicans on their way down the steps.

"Two guys," Bolan said to the crewman as he crawled closer. "One is in the tower, the other is on the bridge roof. You pin down the bridge guy, I'll take the other one. We jump up and shoot on the count of three...."

Then he noticed the way the sailor's hands were shaking. "Are you ready for this?"

The crewman nodded.

At that moment, Bolan had no doubt that he was looking at a nineteen-year-old kid. He knew if he made the sailor stand, the boy would freeze up and die without getting off a shot.

And if he didn't get a shot off, Bolan would die, too.

"Drag that dead guy up here," he told the sailor.

The crewman put down his weapon and descended the stairs. He took hold of the corpse under the arms and grimacing from the weight lugged it up.

"What I want you to do," Bolan said, "is to put the body over your shoulder, and when I give you the signal, throw it over the top step. I don't care how you do it. But get it over and on top of the other body. Got that?"

The sailor nodded. As he swung the corpse up in a fireman's carry, the staircase let out a shrill groan.

But it held.

Bolan braced himself against the wall of the stairway. "Go!" he said.

The crewman had thought the thing through. He rushed to the fourth step from the top then, with a surprising amount of strength, hurled one dead body on top of the other. They collided with a wet smack.

Bolan waited a beat.

As he popped up, exposing himself to enemy fire, the enemy's gunfire riddled the dead body five feet away. He had two distinct targets before him and he'd already decided their order, based on their distance from him and the speed with which each of the shooters could reach hard cover.

He put his sight post under the chin of the guy on the tower and fired four rounds, ending at the guy's head.

Bolan rode the recoil wave to the right and onto his second target.

At this point, the man on the bridge roof had stopped

firing into the dead man's back, but it was too late for him to bring his sights up.

Bolan shot him six times through the chest at a range of no more than twenty feet. By the time the smoking hulls stopped, there wasn't enough left of his heart to fill a matchbox.

Before more opposition could show itself, the Executioner jumped the pile of bodies and flattened himself against the bridge wall. "Get your gun!" he told the sailor. "And tell the others to come on."

It took no more than two minutes for the sailors to climb the stairs and join him.

When they were behind him along the wall, he took hold of the door handle and lifted it. The door wasn't sealed. The latch swung inward.

Bolan rounded the jamb low and fast, with the assault rifle up and ready.

The bridge was deserted. He could see that at once. There was no sign of Yovana Ortiz's boys. Or of their father.

A dead sailor lay sprawled on the floor on the other side of the control console. He had been shot multiple times at close range with an automatic weapon.

The crewmen rushed through the doorway, fanning out to cover the room. Seeing nothing and nobody, they looked at him as if to say, "What next?"

Then heavy gunfire crackled from amidships, and without hesitation, Bolan charged for the opposite door.

23

Juanito jerked violently, startled by the sudden sound of gunfire. The shooting brought back an immediate flood of bad memories of the Murillo brothers' rancho in Baja. And the terror he'd felt when it had come under attack, when it was literally burned down around him. He remembered how the man with the pale blue eyes had saved him and Pedro. The tall stranger had swooped down and stolen them out of the jaws of death like a protecting angel. He couldn't protect their mother at the same time. She had died while the man with blue eyes was flying them back to her.

That man wasn't on the bridge of the ship.

Their father was.

"What the hell?" Samosa said, storming over to the bullet-cracked window. He turned to the two Panamanians standing behind him. "Who's shooting down there? Find out, goddammit!"

The two soldiers looked at each other, as if mentally drawing straws, then one of them slipped out the bridge's port-side door.

A moment passed, then the gunfire got much louder. The crackling and popping doubled in volume.

Pedro edged closer to Juanito, putting his arms around his brother's waist and hiding behind his shoulder and hip. Juanito, who also wanted to hide, had nowhere to go.

When the Panamanian returned to the bridge, out of

breath, he said, "The sailors have broken out of the main hold. They have guns and are moving toward the bow."

"What about Nuñez?" Samosa asked.

"He's fighting at the edge of the bridge deck, along with Salvator and Raimundo. They're holding their own."

"He's still got the damned detonator," the Don said in exasperation.

"What should we do?" said the very pale-faced American named Eames. "If the crew has got control of the middle of the ship, we're trapped up here."

Juanito watched his father, and what he saw amazed him and made him very proud. Though their situation seemed truly terrible, there was no panic in Samosa's eyes. He seemed to draw into himself for a second or two, pulling back to some calm inner place to consider their options. When he was done, he addressed the Panamanians, the gringo and Joseph Crecca.

"We'll wait a couple of minutes and see how things shake out," the drug lord said. "Perhaps our men will be able to subdue the sailors without too much trouble. If they can't, we will have to fight our way back to the stern of the ship to reach the helicopter and boat. In the meantime, seal the bridge doors and keep watch out the windows. Boys, I want you to sit on the couch now and be very still."

Juanito led Pedro by the hand over to the low couch built in to the back wall.

It was very scary. The shooting went on and on as if it would never stop. And not only was there the sharp sound of shooting, but bullets started hitting the back wall of the bridge. The banging noise made Juanito jump every time he heard it. And when he jumped, little Pedro jumped, too.

After what seemed like an hour, but was only a few minutes, the torrent of gunfire raging back and forth seemed to wane. It stopped, then it started. Then it stopped again.

Samosa stepped over to the couch and touched each of their blond heads in turn. "Don't worry, boys," he said to them. "Everything's going to be all right. You'll see. It'll all be over soon."

No sooner had the words escaped his lips than the whole room rocked from a massive explosion outside. The front windows rippled like sheets of water, but they didn't shatter. White tiles from the ceiling rattled loose and fell to the deck.

"We can't stay here any longer, Don Jorge," Crecca insisted. "We've got to make our break while we still can."

Juanito's father was considering this when someone started pounding on the outside of the bridge's port-side door.

"It's Ignacio!" one of the Panamanians cried. "It's Nuñez!"

"Don't just stand there, let him in," Samosa said. "Hurry up!"

When the door swung inward, Nuñez slipped inside. He had some scrapes on his bare legs and he was bleeding from a small cut on his left elbow, but otherwise he seemed okay.

"What's the situation out there?" Samosa demanded.

"The ship's crew tried to take the bridge," the Panamanian replied. "We stopped one part of the force. The other is coming up from the starboard side of the main deck."

"How many?"

Nuñez shrugged. "Hard to say. We killed several that I'm sure of. Could be as many as ten left, but that's just a guess."

"Then we're outnumbered," Crecca said.

"They've got some antiarmor weapons from the ship's arsenal," Nuñez went on. "That was what caused the starboard explosion."

"If that's true, we can't hold out in here," the pale American said. "They'll just blow the doors off."

"Do you have the detonator?" Samosa asked the Panamanian leader.

Nuñez reached into his pocket and pulled out a small electronic device. "Everything is wired and ready to blow whenever you want."

"Good. Can we make it to the stern of this ship without getting trapped by the sailors?"

"If we go along the port side, I think so. Once we reach the stern we can hold them off long enough to abandon ship."

"As soon as we're all clear," Samosa said, "I want you to trigger the charges. Blow the bottom out of it at once. Understand?"

Nuñez smiled. "Yes, Don Jorge."

Everyone in the room flinched as starboard gunfire slammed into the outside of the bridge wall. It sounded like a dozen men were pounding on it with big hammers.

"They're coming up the stairs!" Crecca exclaimed.

"Don't worry," Nuñez said. "Salvator and the others will hold them off for us. They're already in position."

"Out! Move! Everybody!" Samosa shouted. From the top of the control console he picked up a gun. Then he helped Juanito and Pedro to their feet and quickly ushered them across the bridge. As the boys slipped through the doorway on the port side, bullets thundered against the face of the opposite door.

Still tightly clutching Pedro's hand, Juanito led his brother down the stairs, keeping pace with the big men in front of them. When they reached the main deck, the five men and two boys moved in a running column toward the stern.

As they passed under the ship's smokestack, a group of men in dungarees rushed out at them, firing guns.

With a growl, Samosa grabbed Juanito by the shoulder and shoved him down on the deck, which took Pedro down with him. Standing over his boys, standing between them and the flying bullets, the drug lord returned fire. The smoking-hot shell casings rained on Juanito's head and neck, but he was too scared to brush them away, too scared to move. All the men were shooting at once, with the exception of Eames, who was unarmed and cowering on his knees with his arms covering his head.

As Juanito watched from the deck, the men who were attacking them twisted and fell under the hail of bullets, their bodies jerking horribly and then becoming still.

As Samosa hauled Juanito back to his feet, the boy saw another man coming at them from the same direction. In the rush to move on, nobody else seemed to notice him. He was big and he walked with one stiff leg, moving very slowly, though obviously with great effort.

When they reached a stairway leading up the outside of a one-story structure at the back of the ship, they stopped running. Juanito noticed how quiet it was. The shooting had stopped.

Samosa addressed his five surviving soldiers. "Crecca," he said, "get over to the Hatteras, take Eames, Nuñez and his SEALs with you. We'll all meet back in Mazatlán, in the usual place."

The silver-haired man and the Panamanians raced away from them, around the rear corner of the structure.

"Come on, boys," Samosa said. "Up the steps, quickly."

They climbed to the flight deck, which sat atop the low

building. As soon as the helicopter pilot saw them coming across the landing pad, he started the engines.

Samosa opened the rear door and one by one lifted his sons inside.

After he'd buckled them securely into their seats, he turned to the pilot and snarled, "Get us out of here!"

NUÑEZ HAD NO idea that Crecca could run like that. And the American traitor was no slouch, either. He and his men could hardly keep up as the drug cartel underboss and the systems designer sprinted along the helicopter deck. Crecca paused for breath at the corner of the superstructure. Directly across the deck from them was the top of the ladder to the Hatteras. To reach it, they had to cross a firing lane that was only fifteen feet wide.

As they broke from cover, above them, the Sikorsky's engine started turning over with a bone-chilling whine. In the same instant, gunfire sprayed all around them, sparking off the deck and rail.

Nuñez looked to his left at the five men running at them from the bow. The two men in front were shooting.

Nuñez shifted his MP-5 and, without aiming, pinned the trigger, emptying the weapon at them. All he cared about was reaching the top of the ladder and getting over the side, out of the kill zone. He hopped over the rail, onto the steps, right behind the gringo and Crecca.

"Hold them off until we get the motors started," he told the two men who followed.

They didn't argue with him. He was their leader. They knelt on the deck beside the rail and opened fire on the charging sailors.

Below Nuñez, Crecca and Eames had already jumped from the landing to the sport fishing boat. As the Panamanian descended the steps, Crecca scrambled up the ladder to the Hatteras's flying bridge. Eames meanwhile hurled back the rear sliding door to the Hatteras's salon and dived inside, throwing himself down on the floor.

Behind Nuñez, one of his men let out a shrill howl. He looked up to see the man absorb hit after hit in the torso and arms. The impacts spun him around, a complete 360 degrees, then he fell over the side and toppled into the water with a loud splash.

Crecca slapped the vessel's starter and its twin Caterpillar turbos roared to life.

A couple of the sailors stopped running and leaned out over the starboard rail. The bullets they fired along the side of the ship skipped off the steel stairs at Nuñez's heels. They crashed through the front windows of the Hatteras's salon.

The SEAL leader jumped from the foot of the ladder onto the boat's foredeck, then untied the bowline from the landing platform.

"Back off, back off!" he shouted up at the flying bridge.

Crecca frantically worked the binnacle controls. He shifted both engines, grinding the gears, and the vessel reversed away from the *Bernardo Chinle* with a roar.

The Panamanian SEAL who was providing covering fire on the main deck realized at that moment that he was going to be left behind. Tossing down his MP-5, he dived over the rail and off the side of the ship, narrowly missing the front of the ladder as he plummeted. He made a big splash when he hit. Big enough to draw lots of attention.

As he popped up and started to swim madly for the rapidly retreating yacht, gunfire clawed the water around him. The bullets made wet, smacking sounds against his flesh. His arms moved more and more slowly, and then the SEAL stopped swimming and started floating.

Facedown.

Nuñez reached into his pocket and took out the detonator. He armed it with the flick of a switch and raised the antenna.

From the flying bridge, Crecca shifted the engines into forward gear, pounded down the throttles and spun the helm around. As the Hatteras cut a foaming donut in the water, a rain of incoming slugs plowed through its starboard side, chewing up its entire length, splintering fiberglass and crashing out the windows.

As Crecca made his U-turn, Nuñez hopped out on the bow pulpit and did a little victory dance with the detonator raised in his hand.

"Fuck you!" he yelled over at the DIV.

The men along the DIV's rail were firing at him and he didn't care. He put his thumb on the boom button, waiting for the Sikorsky to lift off the ship's flight deck.

BOLAN CHARGED through the bridge's port-side door and over to the staircase leading down to the main deck.

There was no one there, either.

He moved to the end of the bridge wing and leaned over the low perimeter wall, to get a view along the port side of the ship. From this vantage point, he saw the tail end of the file of escaping drug soldiers. They were headed for the stern. Their final destination had to be the helicopter pad and the Hatteras tied on the starboard side. He couldn't see the sailors amidships as they flanked and attacked the retreating thugs, but he heard their gunfire. And the blistering response.

"Back the other way!" he shouted at the sailors behind him. Pushing past them, he ran back through the bridge and out the other door.

They had no choice but to go back the way they had come. Jumping the corpses at the top of the ruined stairs, the Executioner half ran, half slid down the rickety steps. He turned at the landing and slid some more, letting himself fall off the seventh step and land, feetfirst, on the pile of cartel corpses beneath the staircase.

The sailors were right behind him. He hopped out of the way as the next man landed with a grunt on the cushion of dead men.

When the third man hit the deck, a helicopter engine started up at the other end of the ship. As Bolan started running for the stern, he saw a group of drug soldiers crossing the deck, making for the accommodation ladder to the Hatteras. He raised his assault rifle, his finger squeezed on the trigger and the G-3 began spitting death. There was no way he could aim his weapon while running full-tilt. The impacts of his footsteps sent the muzzle jerking, even though he gripped the rifle in both hands.

It didn't matter.

He just wanted to keep the Samosa soldiers off balance while he closed the distance between them.

One of the sailors caught up to him and also started firing as he ran.

Down the deck, a trio of cartel thugs cleared the rail and started down the ladder to the Hatteras. The other two drug soldiers remained on the main deck, where they knelt and returned aimed fire.

At once, the sailor running beside Bolan staggered and stumbled. Something hot and wet sprayed over the Executioner's cheek.

Blood.

Hit in the chest and neck by multiple Parabellum slugs, the sailor stopped running and crashed to the deck, nearly tripping the crewman coming up fast behind.

The second sailor fared no better than the first. Slugs ripped into him immediately, his weapon went flying and he crumpled, rolling head over heels. The drug soldiers at the far end of the ship had the range zeroed in.

Bolan bore down as he ran, walking gunfire along the

aft rail. The sparking bullet strikes climbed over one of the kneeling shooters. The guy stood and took more hits, twisting, then falling over the side.

As his weapon locked back empty, the Executioner heard the Hatteras's engines start.

"Shoot at the boat!" he shouted over his shoulder at the pair of sailors behind him. "Fire on them!"

As he turned his head, a tall figure limped out of a doorway ahead of him.

Bolan ran past Admiral Fuentes. The numbers were falling in a blur. The Hatteras was backing away from the ship.

In front of him, the last kneeling drug soldier jumped overboard, only to be tracked, bracketed and hammered by the crewmen's rifles as he tried to swim away.

Bolan stopped short of the ladder, stripped the spent mag and reloaded. As the Hatteras's bow turned away, it presented itself broadside to the sailors' fire. Even so, the gunner on the bow pulpit was laughing and dancing. Bolan recognized the object he waved in his hand.

Rotor wind beat against the Executioner's back as the helicopter revved, making him squint as he shouldered the G-3 and looked down its sights. Aiming at the man in the pulpit, he fired ten rounds. He held low on purpose and let the muzzle climb drive the bullet strikes up the drug soldier's body.

Eight of the ten shots were body hits.

The last two took off the top of his head.

As the soldier toppled over the pulpit's rail, he let go of the detonator. The vessel threw a rooster tail of water as it roared over his body and the sinking detonator.

The Executioner discarded the G-3 and unslung the LAW. His hands moved quickly, efficiently. It was a ritual they knew by heart.

"Stand aside," Fuentes ordered him. He already had his own LAW launcher extended and ready to fire.

As Bolan sidestepped out of the way, the admiral shouldered the tube and moved the safety handle to Arm.

A second later, the 66 mm rocket screamed away. Its corkscrew smoke trail led right into the stern of the Hatteras. The forty-two-foot boat exploded in an enormous, billowing fireball. Everything that was inside the boat was suddenly outside the boat, in very small pieces. And the man on the flying bridge was swallowed up in the blink of an eye.

Behind them, the Sikorsky started to lift off the pad.

Bolan turned with the extended LAW half raised to his shoulder. As the helicopter banked away from the DIV, he saw inside the cockpit for a split second. He saw two small, frightened faces in the window of the rear compartment.

The Executioner lowered the LAW launcher.

"What are you doing?" Fuentes yelled at him. "Why don't you fire? Give it to me, I'll do it!"

Bolan said nothing.

The admiral was outraged. "Are you crazy? That's Don Jorge Samosa up there. The Lords of the Seas is in your sights!"

"There are also two children on board."

"And how many tens of thousands of innocent lives will Samosa destroy if we don't shoot him down? We may never get this chance again."

Bolan was unmoved.

"I'm going to give the order to power up the missile guidance system," Fuentes said. "There's still plenty of time to launch the ASROCs. Even when he's past the horizon line, they can score a direct hit."

"Sit down," the Executioner told him. For emphasis,

he swung the LAW tube onto his shoulder and pointed its barrel at the admiral's chest.

Fuentes looked at him incredulously.

Up the rail, the other seamen were just as astonished. They stood frozen in place.

"Either you're crazy, or Samosa's bought you off," Fuentes said.

"Wrong on both counts," Bolan said. "The question here is, do the lives of two good human beings outweigh the life of one very bad one?"

"Obviously your answer is yes," Fuentes said, furiously.

"Sit down, Admiral, and take the load off that busted knee."

Bolan looked past the Mexican officer at the rapidly disappearing helicopter. To shoot it down would have been to admit that there was no hope in the world.

And the Executioner could not continue to fight if he believed that.

As he watched the Sikorsky fade into the yellow haze on the horizon, he said, "I'll see you soon."

STONY MAN® 48

Conflict Imperative

In order to end a long war with internal terrorist factions, Peru agrees to hand over part of her sovereign territory to a rebel coalition. The deal is brokered by a reformed IRA terrorist, who is up for a Nobel prize for his peacemaking efforts. But the man has his own agenda, and Bolan is taken prisoner!

Available in August 2000 at your favorite retail outlet.

James Axler

OUTLANDERS®

HELL RISING

A fierce bid for power is raging throughout new empires of what was once the British Isles. The force of the apocalypse has released an ancient city, and within its vaults lies the power of total destruction. Kane must challenge the forces who would harness the weapon of the gods to wreak final destruction.

JAMES AXLER
DEATH LANDS®
Rat King

Emerging into one of the preDark installations known as redoubts, the group is taken prisoner in a fully functioning army base operating in a parody of life before the blowout. Its occupants are inbred soldiers, a legacy to the lost secrets of the Totality Concept. Led by the mad general of an obscene military project, the base has found its last hope in the ragtag bunch.